The Original Big Hair Girls

To Phyllis,
   From one big hair girl to another —
Let the good times roll.
          Love,
   Stella Cooper Mitchell

Walking Ivy's Path

The Original Big Hair Girls

A Novel

Stella Cooper Mitchell

iUniverse, Inc.
New York Lincoln Shanghai

The Original Big Hair Girls

Copyright © 2007 by Stella Cooper Mitchell

All rights reserved. No part of this book may be used or reproduced by any means, graphic, electronic, or mechanical, including photocopying, recording, taping or by any information storage retrieval system without the written permission of the publisher except in the case of brief quotations embodied in critical articles and reviews.

iUniverse books may be ordered through booksellers or by contacting:

iUniverse
2021 Pine Lake Road, Suite 100
Lincoln, NE 68512
www.iuniverse.com
1-800-Authors (1-800-288-4677)

Because of the dynamic nature of the Internet, any Web addresses or links contained in this book may have changed since publication and may no longer be valid.

This is a work of fiction. All of the characters, names, incidents, organizations, and dialogue in this novel are either the products of the author's imagination or are used fictitiously.

Cover design by Michael Dyson

ISBN: 978-0-595-47599-5 (pbk)
ISBN: 978-0-595-91868-3 (ebk)

Printed in the United States of America

To the people that made this book possible, to the people who buy this book, to the people who laugh when they read this book, many thanks.

Chapter 1

Hell, Reform School, and the Pore House

There were three places where I knew I never wanted to be: Hell, reform school, or the "pore" (poor) house.

Every Sunday I went to church to save my soul from Hell. The preacher would tell the girls that if they tempted the boys by wearing makeup, short skirts, pants, or tight sweaters, or if they cut their hair short, they were surely going to Hell. I didn't want that to happen, but the desire to look pretty overruled my righteousness.

Mama kept me on the straight and narrow path by using guilt and the threat of reform school. She would say, "You better finish your supper. You know, there are children in China who are starving to death." I have saved many starving Chinese children by cleaning my plate.

I never got spankings. Mama's guilt trips were enough to keep me in line.

Reform school was one of Mama's favorite threats. She didn't have to really threaten me—she would just point out the wildest girl in high school and say, "If I had a trashy young'n like that, I'd put her in reform school!"

I was very, very good. I sure didn't want to go to reform school!

Once or twice I pushed my sweet Mama to the point of saying, "Sadie Rose Marie Songbird, I'm a good mind to put you in reform school."

When she said this, Jo Lee was usually involved.

I never saw a poor house, but I guess there was one in Nashville. I heard a lot about it. When farm folks were extravagant or wasteful, my Grandma Rose Lena would say, "They had better watch out or they'll wind up in the pore house!"

When I would ask for something that she couldn't afford, Grandma Rose Lena would say, "Are you trying to put me in the pore house?"

Thank God we were never poor. You're not poor if you have more than the people around you have, even if that isn't a lot.

Mama worked very hard to make sure I had as much as everybody else.

Actually, I think we should revive the poor house, as pitiful as it was. In my opinion, the poor house is better than *no* house.

Chapter 2

Jo Lee

Jo Lee McGee and I were about as close as two peas in a pod.

Jo Lee was drop dead gorgeous. Having a drop dead gorgeous friend is almost as good as being drop dead gorgeous yourself—maybe even better.

I never had to fight the boys off with a stick, but I always got all kinds of attention, just because I was Jo Lee's friend.

I always had a date, if Jo Lee did. She would say, "I'm not going unless Sadie goes, too."

Every week we would spend the night together, either at my house or at Jo Lee's.

We studied together all of the time. We liked having the reputation of being smart.

Sometimes we studied with Bully, Worth, and Hadley. Worth was probably the smartest of all of us, especially in science. Hadley was a smart ass and homely looking, but he did have a car.

Along about midnight, when we studied together, we would get hungry and extremely silly.

We would get out the Spam and make Spam and lettuce sandwiches on light bread.

Next came the singing. Our favorite was, *Glorious*. "Glo-reee-us, glo-reee-eee-ous, glo-reee-eee-eee-ous," we'd sing as we scarfed down our sandwiches.

About this time, Mama would stumble out and tell Bully, Worth, and Hadley to go on home.

"Now, girls," she would say to Jo Lee and me, "If you don't know your lesson by now, you aren't ever going to know it! Ya'll get on up to bed, now. You know I have to go to work tomorrow!"

We would go to bed, grumbling, "We're going to fail! I just know we're going to fail!

The next day we would take the test and get our normal "A".

High school was the last time that I've been one of the smartest in the class. I love that feeling.

Chapter 3

Bully

Bully Bower lived right across the street from me. I liked Bully just fine, as a friend, but I didn't want him as a boy friend. He wasn't cute enough. He had one leg that was just a little shorter than the other, and he walked with a slight limp. His lips were way too thick, and his hair was greasy.

Bully's daddy sold produce, and Bully had to work with him a lot.

I kept my cousin's children after school, and one of them was a royal pain in the ass.

I had commented to Mama that Bully was as ugly as they come, and I wanted him to leave me alone. Sipherd overheard me.

Bully was helping his daddy sell a truck load of watermelons on the square in Pea Ridge. A few of the farmers who had come to town had bought a watermelon. They sliced it, salted the pieces, and were seeing how far they could spit the seeds.

Sipherd was with his mama, who was buying a watermelon. "You better leave Sadie alone, 'cause she don't like you, and she said you're ugly, too," Sipherd announced very loudly, for all to hear.

Bully turned beet red, and he was embarrassed, but he didn't say anything.

He stayed away from me and Jo Lee for about a week. His ego was bruised, but eventually he forgave me. Then, he got even.

Bully's daddy got a brand new Edsel as soon as Bully was sixteen. Bully would take Hadley, Worth, Jo Lee, and me for rides. That big old car would fly! We would jump hills at 90 miles per hour.

One weekend, about Thanksgiving, Jo Lee and I went out with Bully to cut Jo Lee a Christmas tree. We went out in the country to a farm where the farmer had told Bully's daddy they could get a Christmas tree.

We found the perfect tree, down in the woods and across a creek. Bully had brought his hatchet and hand saw, and we got the tree cut down in just a few minutes.

Bully dragged the tree back to the car and put it in the trunk while Jo Lee and I stayed behind to gather up some mistletoe.

Bully came back to where we were, and he started helping us pick up the mistletoe that we had piled up on the ground. All of a sudden, Bully took a wrong step and turned his ankle. He couldn't walk, so Jo Lee and I had to pick him up and carry him back to the car.

I had Bully's feet, and Jo Lee had his shoulders. We struggled and panted and sweated to get Bully back to the car. Jo Lee and I got thoroughly soaked when we had to carry Bully across the creek.

We finally got back to the car, and Bully stretched out on the back seat.

I drove back to Jo Lee's house, and the two of us managed to get the tree up on her porch.

Bully limped around to the driver's side of the car.

"My ankle's feeling better," he said. "I think I can drive on home, now."

A year or so later, I learned that Bully was faking it with his ankle, and this was my payback for what Sipherd had said at the watermelon truck.

Chapter 4

Hadley

Hadley's daddy was a hellfire and damnation preacher. He had no idea what Hadley was doing when he was not around the house.

Hadley was chubby. He would pull his belt as tight as he could, so he could say that he wore 34-in-the-waist pants. He looked like a pillow tied in the middle.

I know how mean this was to him, but Hadley had the nickname of "Tater" because he just loved potatoes.

In the eyes of his mama and daddy, Tater could do no wrong. When he got out of their sight, though, that was a different story. Tater would lie like a dog. The only reason that Jo Lee and I put up with him was because he was so smart.

He spread the rumor that he had kissed Jo Lee. This made Jo Lee and me so mad that we could have killed him. Everybody knew this was a lie. Jo Lee was a nice girl, and she hardly ever kissed anybody, especially Tater.

This didn't stop Brother Wright from preaching about wild girls tempting his Hadley by wearing tight sweaters and make up. He said that Hadley couldn't even concentrate on his studies because the girls were tempting him with their wild ways.

Another thing that Tater lied about was the *Playboy* magazine and how it got under his mattress.

Hadley said that he didn't know how the *Playboy* got there, and then he said that Bully was trying to get him in trouble. Hadley's story was that Bully had left the *Playboy* there the last time they spent the night together. Hadley said that he thought he and his daddy needed to pray for Bully.

They prayed for Bully, and then Brother Wright got in his car and went over to Bully's house. Brother Wright told Bully's daddy about the trash that Bully had left at his house. Poor Bully got a whipping for something that he wasn't even guilty of.

Chapter 5

Blind Talley

Once a month, Trudy left Miller in charge of the other children and took Mama, Jo Lee, and me to Nashville. We loved to go shopping at Harvey's.

This was a wonderful treat for Mama and me. We didn't get to go to Nashville much. Mama didn't drive, and at that time, we didn't have a car. We had to rely on our feet and on other people to drive us around. Thank God we lived in town!

Every time we went to Harvey's, we had to pass by Blind Talley. The first time Jo Lee and I passed by Blind Talley, we were little girls, about six years old. Jo Lee put some money in his cup, and she made me put some in, too.

Jo Lee always put money in Blind Talley's cup. She also did a lot of crying. Jo Lee was very tender hearted.

I didn't have much money to spend, but Jo Lee would make me put a whole dollar in Blind Talley's cup every time we went to Nashville.

Blind Talley sat on the sidewalk against the wall of a building. He didn't have legs below his knees, and he had a wooden platform with wheels on it to roll himself around.

He wore sun glasses and a long overcoat in every season of the year. He played a guitar by resting the back on his thighs, strumming it with his right hand, and sliding over the frets with a bottle neck that he wore on his left index finger. Every time we heard him, Blind Talley was playing and singing the blues.

Jo Lee always said that Blind Talley had every right to play and sing the blues, because he didn't have any legs and he couldn't see.

One time, when we were walking to Harvey's, we passed Blind Talley's usual spot, but he wasn't there.

Jo Lee started sobbing, "Blind Talley's dead! Blind Talley's dead!"

"Maybe he's just in the hospital," I said.

"Maybe he's visiting his children or his mama," Mama said.

"Blind Talley doesn't have kids or a mother," Jo Lee said.

"How do you know that?" asked Trudy.

"Because he doesn't have any legs," said Jo Lee.

"That has nothing to do with it," Trudy said. "I've told you the facts of life."

This made Jo Lee so mad. "Mu-ther", she sighed, as she rolled her eyes.

As we turned the corner, a man wearing a long overcoat and sun glasses, carrying a guitar and a tin cup, walked right into us. It was Blind Talley, and he recognized some of his regular customers.

"Praise God, the Lord has healed me! I can walk again," was all Blind Talley had to say.

The next time we went to Harvey's, there sat Blind Talley, playing his guitar, with his cup at the ready. Jo Lee put some money in the cup, but I saved my dollar to buy fudge. Jo Lee never said a word.

I knew Blind Talley just couldn't grow his legs back!

Chapter 6

Beans, Beans, Everywhere and Not a Bite to Eat

Mama raised me alone from the time I was twelve years old.

There wasn't anything Mama couldn't take care of, one way or another. She had to be quite creative a lot of times. We didn't have any money to waste.

Mama worked as a switchboard operator to support us.

She knew all kinds of ways to save money. She always made a garden in our back yard. She tilled the land herself, then planted and harvested the vegetables. Then, she canned them in the pressure cooker. This provided us with most of our food. It was good and also healthy. Mama was a wonderful cook!

Mama could fix things when they broke. There was no such thing as "getting a new one".

"Waste not, want not," was her motto. Another motto was, "A penny saved is a penny earned."

Mama could sew beautifully. I had cuter clothes than most girls, and more of them.

Mama could also cut hair. I always had the newest hair style, and I didn't have to pay a cent for it. My hair is naturally curly, so I never needed a permanent wave, and I never had to suffer the results of a "dandelion head" because of some hair stylist.

Mama was very easy-going, most of the time. I could do almost everything I wanted to.

Once in a while, though, I would make Mama really mad. Jo Lee was usually involved. This is one thing that happened.

Mama was canning green beans in the pressure cooker. Green beans were everywhere—it was a bumper crop that year. Snapped green beans were on the kitchen counter, bushel baskets of unsnapped green beans were on the floor, and the pressure cooker was full of glass jars filled with green beans.

Mama ran out of jar lids, and she told Jo Lee and me that she was going to Era Ogan's house to borrow some lids.

"Now girls, be sure and watch those green beans carefully. I've been having trouble with my pressure cooker. The minute you hear the first jiggle of the pressure cooker, turn the stove eye down to low heat. I'll be back in a minute."

"Sure, Mama," we said.

In about five minutes we heard a knock at the door. It was Ricky Van Clark, one of the cutest boys in school. Jo Lee wanted to go out with him so bad!

We went to the door together. When we saw who was there, we forgot all about the pressure cooker.

Ricky Van Clark needed help with an algebra problem. Jo Lee was happy to help him. They sat side by side on the sofa, working out the problem. I sat in a chair, hoping Ricky Van Clark would ask Jo Lee out. Then, a terrible explosion happened.

"Hit the floor! The Russians have bombed us," I shouted.

Ricky Van Clark grabbed his algebra book and started running. Jo Lee and I got up off the floor and ran after him through the door.

Neighbors started coming out of their houses to see what had happened. I started shouting again, "The Russians have bombed us!"

About that time, Mama came running out of Era Ogan's house.

"Are you alright?" she asked Jo Lee and me.

"I think so," Jo Lee said.

"We need to call President Eisenhower," I yelled.

"Shut up, Sadie Rose Marie Songbird," exclaimed Mama. "The Russians aren't coming, and we don't need the army. Ya'll have let my pressure cooker explode!"

I knew that Jo Lee and I were in real trouble. Mama never called me by my entire, full name, unless it was serious.

We went back in the house to survey the damage. A dozen neighbors followed us.

The damage was bad, no question about it. Beans and glass were everywhere—on the walls, the ceiling, the floor, and the cabinets. There was a huge hole in the ceiling where the pressure cooker top had hit.

We started cleaning up that big old mess. The neighbors pitched right in and helped.

"Sadie Rose Marie, I ought to send you to reform school," Mama said. "I told you to watch my beans. Why didn't you mind me?"

"She didn't mean to forget about them. It was all my fault," said Jo Lee.

"You shut up, too, Jo Lee! I'm calling Trudy," shouted Mama. "You two could have been killed!"

Mama was crying and sweeping up beans and glass at the same time.

"You're fixing every bit of this! Get a rag and start washing. This winter, when we have nothing to eat and you're hungry, you'll wish you'd watched my beans," cried Mama.

I started to say that we could just eat corn, but I thought about that and just kept my mouth shut.

A sheriff's car pulled up out front. The sheriff and Ricky Van Clark got out of the car.

Ricky Van Clark said, "The Russians bombed Sadie's house! Go arrest them!"

"Lou Zena's going to send Sadie to reform school," said Myrtle, one of our neighbors.

Trudy drove up about that time and came running in the house. "Jo Lee! Sadie! Lou Zena! Are you all alright?" she hollered.

"We're fine," said Mama. "After we get this mess cleaned up, I want you to take Sadie home with you. I'm afraid I'm going to kill her!"

"Now, settle down," said the sheriff. "Where's them Russians that bombed your house?"

"You stupid bastard," Mama exploded. "There are no Russians here! Sadie and Jo Lee just blew up the pressure cooker!"

"Lou Zena Songbird, you shouldn't call me a stupid bastard," said the sheriff. I'm a good mind to slap these handcuffs on you and take you to jail."

"Sheriff, she's sorry she called you a stupid bastard," said Trudy. "She's just real upset! We really don't need you here anymore, since there aren't any Russians here. Just go on, now, and we'll be fine when we get this mess cleaned up."

"Humph," said the sheriff, as he hitched up his britches and his gun belt, sniffed, and sauntered toward the door.

"Sadie, get your clothes together. You're going home with me," said Trudy.

As we walked outside, Mama was still mumbling to herself. "Couldn't be any dumber if your head was cut off! Could have put your eye out!"

Chapter 7

Sapphire

I always felt so sorry for Sapphire Bingaman. She was pretty, but not nearly as pretty as her little sister and her mama. She was hard of hearing and because of this, very shy.

Sapphire's mama, Lucille, was movie-star-pretty, with long, jet black hair, light blue eyes, and a perfect size seven figure. She spent a lot of money on her clothes and makeup. She drove around town in a 1957 turquoise blue Ford convertible.

I wasn't allowed to go to Sapphire's house, but Mama liked her, and she could come to my house any time she wanted to.

The gossip around town was that Lucille was a "loose woman". In reality, all she did was to have a very long affair with a policeman who lived in Nashville.

Neither Sapphire nor Sissy was Lee Roy Bingaman's natural child. Branton Newton, Lucille's high school sweetheart, was their father. When Lucille told Branton that she was pregnant, he ran away for two months.

In those days, girls were treated like dirt if they were unmarried with a baby.

Lucille knew she had to do something fast.

Lee Roy Bingaman had always loved Lucille from afar, and he asked her to marry him. Out of desperation, this is what she did.

Branton came back to town to marry Lucille a week after she married Lee Roy. Branton was heartbroken. He went to Nashville and enrolled in the police academy, hoping somebody would shoot him—but that never happened. Lucille kept on having her affair with Branton, even though she was married to Lee Roy.

Jo Lee and I loved to go to Sapphire's house, even though I wasn't allowed to go there. We would tell our mamas that we were going to the library to study, and then we would walk on over to Sapphire's house.

Lucille was so much fun! She would help us with our makeup and give us new hairdos. She could really cut a rug, and she taught us all the new dance steps.

When we were feeling really brave, Lucille would put the top down on her convertible and ride us all around town, or take us to Pat's Drive-in.

Sapphire's daddy was never at home. He drove an eighteen-wheeler rig from Tennessee to California, hauling pigs and moonshine. Lee Roy wasn't a bad man—he just had no idea about how to be a daddy.

Lee Roy paid very little attention to any of his family. Lucille could get by with her affair with Branton as long as Lee Roy wasn't home. Lee Roy kept them supplied with plenty of money, and he left everything else up to Lucille.

I don't think that Lucille was careful enough about her affair, because Lee Roy came home once, unexpectedly, and found Lucille and Brandon together. He told both of them that if he ever caught them together again, he'd shoot them both.

Well, not long after that, Lee Roy came home unexpectedly again. Branton was there with Lucille—but so was I, Jo Lee, and about a half-dozen other girls. Branton and Lucille were teaching us dance steps.

This was too much for Lee Roy to take. He went outside to his eighteen-wheeler and got his gun. He came back inside and shot Lucille in the head. Then, he wounded Branton in the arm.

This scared Jo Lee and me half to death. We took off running and didn't stop until we were at my house.

"What's wrong, girls," Mama asked. "You look like you just saw a ghost."

Jo Lee and I knew we would be in terrible trouble if we told the truth, but we didn't have time to make up a good story.

At the same time, Jo Lee said, "We saw a snake," and I said, "We almost got run over by a truck."

Mama said, "There's blood on both of you. You'd better be telling me the truth, because I'm calling the law."

We knew we had better tell the truth, no matter what. We told Mama to call the sheriff and an ambulance.

"Sapphire's mama is dead, and so is Branton," said Jo Lee.

"Mama, I know you're going to kill us, and that's what we deserve. We weren't at the library like we told you—we were at Sapphire's house," I said.

"Hello, sheriff, this is Lou Zena Songbird. Lucille Bingaman and Branton Newton are dead at Lucille Bingaman's house."

"We're on our way," said the sheriff. "We've got an ambulance on the way, too."

Mama looked at Jo Lee and me. We were so scared. We were shaking and crying.

"I'm so sorry we lied to you about the library," I bawled.

"We'll deal with your lying later," said Mama. "Right now, just tell me exactly what happened. Are you both alright?" Mama was crying, herself, and hugging us.

"Well," I said, "we were all at Sapphire's house—Jo Lee, me, and six other girls. We were eating potato chips and drinking Cokes. Lucille and Branton were teaching us new dance steps. Sapphire's daddy came home, and I guess he was mad because Branton Newton was there. He went back outside to his truck and got his gun and shot them."

Mama called Trudy. "Trudy, get over here as fast as you can! Something awful has happened!"

"Are the girls alright?" asked Trudy.

"Yes, they're fine right now. They may not be later," said Mama.

"What's wrong?" asked Trudy.

"Sapphire's mother is dead," said Mama. "I'll tell you all about it when you get here. Now, hurry!"

Trudy came screeching to a halt in front of our house. Mama, Jo Lee, and I crawled in the car. Trudy took off for Sapphire's house. It took us about three minutes to get there. Trudy was flying!

When we got to Sapphire's house, police cars were everywhere, and almost everybody who lived in town was in the front yard, milling around.

Mama and Trudy grabbed our hands and pushed through the crowd. We went in the house, and poor little Sapphire and Sissy were huddled together in a corner.

"Get your things together," Trudy said to them.

"We're taking you home with us," Mama said.

"I want my Mama," cried Sissy.

"I know," said Mama.

Trudy dropped all four of us off at home. Then, she and Mama took off for the hospital.

We were all crying, and at the same time, trying to make Sapphire and Sissy feel better.

In about an hour, Mama and Trudy came home.

"Sapphire, Sissy—your mama isn't dead. As a matter of fact, she's just fine," said Mama.

"What about Branton?" asked Sissy.

"He's fine, too," said Mama.

"But Daddy shot Mama in the head," Sapphire wrote on her note pad. Sapphire could talk, but she preferred to write.

"The bullet barely grazed the top of her skull. They already have her sewn up, and she's just fine, I promise you," said Trudy.

"Branton has a bullet wound in his arm. He's fine, too," said Mama.

"Daddy! What about Daddy?" asked Sissy.

"He's in jail, charged with attempted murder," said Mama. "I think he'll get off scot free because of the circumstances."

"You girls are going to spend the night here, and your mama will pick you up tomorrow," Mama continued.

Lucille looked awful the next day, when she came to pick up Sapphire and Sissy.

"You ought to be ashamed of yourself," said Mama. "You need to take better care of these sweet little girls."

"I know," said Lucille. "I'm going to make some changes in my life, starting today."

Jo Lee and I didn't even get in trouble. I think Mama and Trudy were so thankful that we were alright that they decided we had gotten enough punishment by witnessing an attempted murder.

One thing for sure—we never went to Sapphires's house again.

True to her word, Lucille made a change for the better. She divorced Lee Roy and married Branton.

Chapter 8

Here Comes Trouble

White Gibbs got his name, Trouble, when he was four years old. He pulled old Miss Drinkall's tomato plants up. The next day he pulled Lettie Banks' flowers up. The day after that, he pulled Miss Drinkall's tomato plants up again.

Trouble's Mama and Daddy were old. They couldn't do one thing with him. When they tried, he stood still and screamed at the top of his lungs until he got his way.

Trouble was born with something wrong with his spleen. If you even bumped into him, he got the biggest bruise you ever saw. I don't think I ever saw him without two black eyes.

He took full advantage of his disorder, and he got away with all kinds of things. But his growing up years were nothing, compared to his teen-age years. No parent would let their daughter go out with him—not that the girls would want to. Even the unfortunate looking girls steered clear of Trouble.

He wrecked his parent's car—twice. They banned him from driving their car anymore, but that didn't stop him. He just stole it. He drove to Nashville, picked up a working girl, and wound up in jail.

Jo Lee knew his reputation, but she felt sorry for him. She invited him to her house, and of course, I was there.

Actually, Trouble could be quite charming when he wanted to.

Jo Lee made brownies, and we sat around, talking, eating brownies, and drinking Cokes. Trudy wasn't home, and she didn't know that Jo Lee had invited Trouble to her home. She wouldn't have stood for that.

Trouble told us such sad stories about his life that he almost made us cry. He told us that he only had three years to live, and he told us that his parents hated him and beat him all the time. "Why do you think I have black eyes all the time?" he asked.

Jo Lee said, "Well, I heard you had a spleen disease."

"No," said Trouble. "My parents just hit me."

"Don't they know they could kill you?" I asked.

"They don't care," he whined.

"We heard that you stole their car," I said.

"I did not! That's a big lie," he whined some more, and he convinced us.

We thought, "He's a nice boy, and we're going to help him make friends."

Trouble could talk the Devil into putting out the fire in Hell.

"Where is your bathroom, Jo Lee?" he asked.

"Just down the hall on the right."

He came back in a few minutes. "Well, I'd better be going," he said.

"Oh, stay a little longer," said Jo Lee. "Mama won't be home for a while."

Trudy would have thrown a fit if she knew that White Gibbs was in her house.

"White Gibbs is trouble," she had often told us. "Stay away from him!"

White ran out of the front door and got in the car that he often stole from his parents.

"See you later, alligator," he yelled, as the car kicked up dust down the driveway.

The next day, Trudy discovered that all of her jewelry was missing.

"Jo Lee, do you know anything about my jewelry? Do you know where it is?"

"No, Mama," she replied. "I haven't seen any of it."

"Well, come back here and help me look for it," Trudy answered.

Jo Lee, Trudy, and I searched the whole house. There wasn't a single piece of jewelry to be found.

Jo Lee and I looked at each other, and we knew we had to tell Trudy the truth.

"Mama," Jo Lee said, "White Gibbs was here yesterday. I'll bet he stole it."

"I'll deal with you later," said Trudy. "Right now, I have to call the law."

The deputy sheriff came out to Jo Lee's house, and we told him our story. He had no doubt that Trouble had stolen Trudy's jewelry. The police had to go to Trouble's house at least once a week to check on one report or the other.

"Why did you let him in your house?" asked the deputy.

"I didn't," said Trudy. "Jo Lee and Sadie did. I'm going to deal with them!"

The deputy got to Trouble's house before he had time to get rid of Trudy's jewelry. She got every piece of it back.

Trudy didn't let Jo Lee and me off the hook, though. We had to go to Jo Lee's great aunt's farm for a week and do some hard work.

Trouble finally got what was coming to him. He was the only person I ever knew who actually got sent to reform school.

Chapter 9

▼

Farm Hands

Our punishment for letting Trouble in Trudy's house was to go to Jo Lee's great aunt Mazie's farm for a week of hard labor.

Nothing is harder than hard labor on a farm!

Uncle Leo came by Trudy's house one Monday morning in his pickup truck to take us to the farm.

The first day wasn't hard, though. We watered Aunt Mazie's flowers which she grew in tin cans. We asked her why she used tin cans and not flower pots. She said, "Because tin cans are free."

After we watered the flowers, we sat on the front porch and snapped green beans. Then, we hand-churned butter. We helped cook what Aunt Mazie called "dinner" that they ate in the middle of the day. "Dinner" was in the middle of the day and "supper" was at night.

Dinner was absolutely delicious. We had ham, fresh snap beans, fried corn, fried okra, mashed potatoes, a dodger of corn bread, biscuits, and banana pudding.

After dinner, Aunt Mazie threw a tablecloth over the food on the table. Later on, we found out why.

That afternoon we worked on a quilt and gathered eggs. "This isn't bad at all," said Jo Lee.

Wrong! Wrong! Wrong!

That evening we had to get the cows up from the pasture to the barn and milk them. That was no fun at all! We didn't know how to milk a cow. Jo Lee's cow kicked her off the stool she was sitting on and she fell in a cow pie. My cow beat the crap out of my face with her tail. Then, I stepped in a cow pie with my new slippers on.

When we finally got the cows milked, and we got back to the house, Aunt Mazie took the tablecloth off the food we had at dinner and that was our supper—cold everything! Grease was standing on top of all the vegetables.

"If you don't like what we have to eat for supper, just have some corn bread and buttermilk," said Aunt Mazie.

We sure didn't want that.

After supper, we gathered around the radio. Uncle Leo found WLAC in Cincinnati, Ohio, and we listened to songs for a couple of hours. One I definitely remember was Little Jimmy Dickens singing, "Take an Old Cold 'Tater and Wait". Jo Lee and I started feeling sorry for ourselves, and we went to bed hungry.

The next day, Uncle Leo and Aunt Mazie woke us up before daylight to help with the milking, again. But before we went out to the barn, I had to empty the slop jar. They didn't have an inside bathroom, and during the day we had to use the outhouse. At night we used a slop jar, and that had to be emptied every morning, so I got the "slop jar job".

When we went out to the barn, Jo Lee and I just went barefooted. You couldn't see in the half-light of dawn, and I stepped on a rake. The handle hit me right between my eyes, and it made a big knot on my forehead. When I rubbed it, it felt like a big pumpkin.

When we started milking, the cows beat the crap out of us again with their tails.

Aunt Mazie called us in for breakfast, and we were starving, since we hadn't had much supper the night before. Breakfast was larruping good: homemade sack sausage, gravy, hot homemade biscuits, fried eggs, molasses, and butter.

We stirred our molasses and butter together and sopped our biscuits in it. We weren't allowed to do that at home—we had to use good manners.

Aunt Mazie heated water on the wood stove, and we took a bath in a wash pan. We realized how fortunate we were to have modern conveniences at home.

Aunt Mazie and Uncle Leo had electricity, but it was minimal—bare light bulbs hanging from the ceiling and a few outlets. The running water was one faucet in the kitchen. It ran cold water all of the time, and you couldn't turn it off.

After Jo Lee and I got dressed, Aunt Mazie handed each of us a bonnet and an apron. She told us to go to the garden and pick beans, corn, okra, and tomatoes. After we did that, she said, we could dig potatoes.

That was back breaking work. We were dirty again and sweating, and I hate to sweat!

Dinner was delicious. We ate a lot because we knew what supper would be.

After dinner we wanted to take a nap, but Aunt Mazie would have no part of that. We were free help, and she was taking full advantage.

"Get your buckets," she said. "You're going blackberry picking."

She told us where the blackberry patch was and sent us on our way.

The sun was bearing down on us. We got scratched from head to toe on the blackberry briars, and sweat got in our scratches and in our eyes. We were miserable.

We went back to the house with half a bucket of blackberries each.

"This won't even make a pie," said Aunt Mazie. "Have a dipper full of cool water, and then get back out there and pick at least five buckets of berries."

"Five buckets full!" exclaimed Jo Lee. "Aunt Mazie, I think you're trying to kill us!"

"No, I'm not," she replied. "Your Mama told me about you letting trash in her house and how he stole all her jewelry. I'm trying to teach you a lesson."

I hate lessons!

Five buckets later, we came back to the house. We nearly had sunstroke, we were red faced, and we were wringing wet with sweat. But the worse thing was the chiggers.

They had gotten in around our panty legs. Scratching was not an option for us because we were "raised right"—but if you've got chiggers, you're going to scratch!

Chapter 10

▼

Wheels

The absolute only thing I was better at than Jo Lee was driving. Driving and Jo Lee did not mix.

Back then, there was no such thing as "driver's ed". Your daddy taught you—or, in our case, Trudy.

Trudy was way ahead of her time. She had her own car, a brand spanking new Buick. Trudy would take us out in the country and let us drive. Jo Lee would beg Trudy to not make her drive, but I loved it.

The final straw came when Jo Lee was driving. Jo Lee was making the car creep along. Both of her hands were on the steering wheel, and her eyes were glued on the road. Then, a cat came out of nowhere, and it dashed right in front of us. Jo Lee jerked the steering wheel to miss the cat and wrapped Trudy's Buick around a tree. She jumped out of the car to make sure the cat was alive.

Trudy was screaming, "You've ruined my brand new car!"

Jo Lee was looking at the cat. The cat was hissing and slapping at her. That old tom cat was just fine! The crowning moment, though, was when Jo Lee asked Trudy if she could take the cat home.

I knew that Jo Lee was in awful trouble. Trudy was about to have a stroke. "Jo Lee McGee, how could you ask me such a thing? You'll never drive *my* car again! I may just put you in reform school!"

While Trudy was letting off steam, I ran the cat off into the woods. Jo Lee was crying, and I was trying to smooth out the situation. "It's not that bad—it's only the bumper. Look, it's only a little dent. Please, please, don't put Jo Lee in reform school. See, she's sorry—she's making herself miserable with her crying."

I saved Jo Lee that time—but I knew better than to ask Trudy if I could drive home.

The car was fine, and Trudy finally calmed down, but that day ended Jo Lee's driving career. To my knowledge, she has never driven a car again.

She does, however, collect cats. The last time I heard from her, she had six of them.

Chapter 11

▼

Little Bitty

Little Bitty was my other best friend in high school. When she graduated from high school two years before I did, she got a job as a secretary. She bought herself a car, and she lived at home, so she had money *and* wheels.

I introduced her to Jo Lee, and they liked each other, so we all ran around together. Mama loved Little Bitty, so we could come and go as we pleased.

Little Bitty's real name was Casey Jo, but everybody called her "Little Bitty" because she was tiny.

Our favorite pastime was riding around—it's called "cruising" now. We would start at the courthouse square, then we would go down to Pat's Drive-In, and then over to the roller skating rink. Speaking of skating, that was our second favorite thing to do.

I am totally unathletic, so needless to say, skating did not come easy for me. My knee caps are permanently scarred, but I managed to learn to skate.

Curtis lived next door to me in Mama's rental house. He was awesome on skates. Jo Lee, Little Bitty, and I would take turns skating with him. He could dance on skates and skate backwards.

The roller skating rink was a good place to visit with old friends and to make new ones.

I was larger than Casey Jo and Jo Lee—I had big bones—but our wardrobe was interchangeable. I would cinch up my waist with a girdle and put on a long-line padded bra. I was in excessive misery, but I was cute!

The backgrounds of us three girls were basically the same. We were daughters of hard-working, honest, clean, and well-fed people. Our parents gave us values to live by and to fall back on. We would not have dreamed of stepping out of line. Our parents wouldn't stand for that!

I didn't want to go to reform school—that was Mama's favorite threat, so I behaved, most of the time.

Little Bitty took on the role of big sister to Jo Lee and me, so when Mama wasn't around and I was about to get in trouble, Little Bitty would say, "What do you think your mama would say about that?" I would get so mad at her—but I behaved myself.

Little Bitty married her high school sweetheart about the same time that Jo Lee moved to Michigan, so I was left to fend for myself. I still saw Little Bitty a lot, but she loved Donnie more than she loved me.

I was so sad! But then, Mary Grace changed schools, and she needed a friend as much as I did, and we had the same last name. Christina was in our home economics class, and she started helping us with our aprons and with our cooking. Mary Grace and I were not very good at sewing or cooking, and Christina was a master of both.

Christina became our best friend, and to this day we are all fast friends.

Chapter 12

Heartbroken

In our junior year of high school, my beloved Jo Lee moved to Michigan. I thought I might die of a broken heart.

For years, we had studied together, giggled together, and helped each other through all kinds of trouble. We spent the night together at least once a week, and sometimes we stayed an entire week at each other's house.

We cried, I begged for Jo Lee to stay. Mama said she could live with us. Miller and Trudy said, "No way!"

I had to start all over again, finding a best friend. Every girl has to have a best friend.

For a while after Jo Lee left, I went around in a blue funk. Nobody could cheer me up, and people were starting to get tired of me acting the "poor pitiful Pearl" role.

After a couple of weeks, though, I found my new best friends—Mary Grace Songbird and Christina Faith Gooden. Mary Grace and I have the same last name. We found out later that we are distant cousins because Daddy and Mary Grace's daddy are second cousins.

Mary Grace's family moved back to Pea Ridge after they had been gone for about ten years. Mary Grace's daddy had moved to Nashville to work in construction, and now they were back.

Christina's daddy was a Methodist preacher, and the church conference sent them to Pea Ridge. Christina came to town about a week after Mary Grace got here. They were perfect, smart, pretty, kind, and funny.

Life was good again.

Chapter 13

If A Pretty Boy Asks You Out, Run!

Dusty Silvers was the best looking boy who had ever passed through the halls of Pea Ridge High School.

Mary Grace, Christina, and I all wanted to go out with him.

Mary Grace was the prettiest of the three of us, and also the smartest. However, I was the one who did his homework for him for an entire year.

Dusty finally asked me out when his cheerleader girlfriend, Cherry, got mad at him the week before the prom and broke up with him.

We were all excited about my date with Dusty and going to the prom. How lucky could a girl get?

I begged and pleaded with Mary Grace until she agreed to go to the prom with Frankie, a friend of Dusty's. Frankie had a brand new 1960 Chevvy, but he was a shy boy and not very attractive. Dusty hung out with him because Frankie had that new car, and it made Dusty look even cuter.

Frankie's daddy was the mayor of Pea Ridge. Frankie always had plenty of money, and Dusty was always broke. Dusty would borrow money from Frankie and never pay it back.

We had been looking forward to the prom for months. Mama made all of our prom dresses. They were just alike, and we loved to dress alike.

The dresses were pale green chiffon with a cinched waist, full length hoop skirt, and strapless. Hoop skirts are a pain to sit down in, especially in a car.

We lined up kitchen chairs and practiced sitting down like ladies. We didn't want to show our panties. If you accidentally sat down on the hoop, your dress would fly over your head.

Mary Grace and I spent the night before our prom and the day of the prom with Christina.

Christina lived way out in the country, down a dirt road. When it rained a lot, the rainwater would stand for days in mud puddles.

We worked all day long, trying to get beautiful for the prom. We back combed our hair. I put mine in a flip, Mary Grace put hers in a French twist and put a flower in it, and Christina put hers in a bee hive and put a tiny bow in it. We polished our nails, put on pancake makeup, and Tangeé lipstick.

We put on our matching prom dresses and our five-inch high heel shoes. Three beauty queens, ready for the prom.

We waited … and waited … and waited. Finally, Dusty showed up in his grandpa's pickup truck. That was fine with us, because Frankie would drive his new car. Actually, Frankie looked pretty good behind the wheel of his car.

Dusty got out of the pickup and swaggered up to the veranda. Then, he pulled out his comb and slicked back his ducktail. Mary Grace, Christina, and I all swooned.

Christina didn't have a prom date. She was going to stand in the "stag-ette" line in the gym and hope that someone other than Theron Fike would ask her to dance.

Theron would ask all the girls to dance. The problem was, Theron couldn't dance, but he thought he could.

The week before the prom, the decorating committee had decorated the gym to look like Hawaii.

When Dusty knocked on the door, we all answered it. I asked Dusty where Frankie was. Dusty said that he didn't know. He had told Frankie to meet him at Christina's house. "He's probably just running a little late," I thought.

We waited thirty more minutes, and then we realized that Mary Grace had been stood up.

Mary Grace was so mad! It was bad enough to be stood up, but to be stood up by an ugly boy like Frankie was humiliating.

We asked Christina's mama if we could borrow her car. "Absolutely not," she replied.

Dusty said that we would just have to ride in the bed of the truck, or not go to the prom. He said that he would drive slowly so the wind wouldn't mess up our hair.

We really didn't want to do this ... but it *was* Dusty, after all.

All of us got in the back of the truck. Dusty took off like a race horse out of the gate. We had to hold on to the wooden slats on the truck bed to keep from falling off. We met another car on the narrow dirt road, and Dusty had to swerve over to keep from having a head-on collision. He hit an enormous mud puddle and got mired up to the hub caps.

He told us to get out the truck. We did, and he gunned it before we had time to get out of the way. We got covered from head to toe in mud.

At this point, I didn't care how good looking Dusty was—*I hated his guts*!

Dusty said that he would walk down the road and see if he could get somebody to come and help him get the truck out of the mud. Mary Grace, Christina, and I started walking back toward Christina's house.

"I hate Dusty Silvers," I said. "I hope he fails every subject! I'll never do his homework again!"

Christina and Mary Grace agreed with me. Stood up by an ugly boy ... covered from head to toe in mud ... our beautiful prom dresses ruined—we were feeling pitiful.

About that time, George Washington Tucker Green came along in the car that he and Alice Ivy shared. He saw us, stopped, and backed up.

"What on earth happened to you?" he asked.

We told him the whole story.

George had graduated from Pea Ridge High School the year before—the smartest boy to ever graduate from Pea Ridge. At this point in time, though, we didn't care anything about that. What we did care about was—he was a wonderful person.

"I came home for the weekend to wash clothes and help Mama June with her term paper," he said. "Let's give this some thought. Get in the car, and we'll decide what to do."

We tried to get in the car, but our hoop skirts wouldn't fit.

"Take your hoop slips off and put them in the trunk," said George. "I won't look."

We took our hoop slips off, and to our surprise, George really didn't look.

"Let's go to my house," he said. "I think Alice Ivy and Mama will have some dresses that'll do. Then, I'll take you on to the prom, if you want me to."

Chapter 14

Miss Anna Saves the Day

We all loved George's mama. She was our teacher, and everybody wanted to be in Miss Anna's class. Every year she managed, somehow, to move up a grade with George and Alice Ivy, so she could be their teacher. I think she got to do that because Mr. Green (Big Daddy—Miss Anna's father-in-law) was Superintendent of Schools and Miss Lucy (the principal of Pea Ridge High School) was Miss Anna's best friend.

George drove us to his house. Miss Anna and Dr. Pooten were having dinner—*Spam on a Stick*.

"What on earth happened to you girls?" Miss Anna asked.

We told her the whole story, ending with Dusty getting stuck in the mud and spraying us while he was trying to get out.

"Sadie Rose Marie Songbird, you've got no business going out with Dusty Silvers. You can do so much better than that," said Miss Anna.

"But, he's the best looking boy in Pea Ridge High School," I said.

"Looks aren't everything," she replied. "But we'll talk about that later. Right now, let's get you ready for the prom. Go upstairs to the bathroom and get cleaned up, while I find you something to wear."

We took off our beautiful matching prom dresses and started washing the mud off our faces, arms, and shoulders. We did the best we could, getting the mud out of our coffered hair.

George knocked on the door and said, "Hand me your dresses."

We did, and he didn't even try to look.

"Mary Grace, try this—it's Alice Ivy's prom dress from last year," said Miss Anna. "Christina, you try this one. I wore it to a teacher's conference, and I think it'll do for you. Sadie, I'm still trying to find you something. Girls, you'll find my makeup in the drawer in the bathroom. Get your makeup on!"

Mary Grace and Christina put on their dresses. They were beautiful, and they fit perfectly.

"Sadie, this is the best I can do for you," said Miss Anna. She handed me a dress that I remembered Alice Ivy had worn when she graduated from the eighth grade. I almost cried because it had puffed sleeves.

"Come on out, and let me see how you look," said Miss Anna. "Mary Grace … Christina … you look wonderful. Sadie … that dress will never do! Let me think. Sadie, you may have to start a new trend."

Dr. Pooten was waiting patiently downstairs.

"John, go to your house and bring me that table cloth you just bought," said Miss Anna.

"But why, Anna?" he asked.

"Just do it, and hurry!" she snapped. "George, go downstairs and bring me that roll of Christmas ribbon, every safety pin you can find, and the scissors."

"What for?" George asked.

"We're making a dress, that's why. Now hurry! I don't want these girls to miss all of the prom."

Dr. Pooten came back about ten minutes later with four table cloths. For the life of me, I didn't know why we needed a table cloth.

Miss Anna picked the prettiest table cloth—damask, with lace overlay. She started to cut the table cloth right down the middle.

"Anna, have you lost your mind?" Dr. Pooten asked. "That table cloth cost $5.95!"

"Just quiet down, John," Miss Anna replied. "I know what I'm doing."

Miss Anna wrapped the half table cloth around me and started pinning me in it. Then, she cut satin chiffon ribbon and told everybody to start tying bows up and down my back. Next, she took a wide satin ribbon and tied it around my waist. That turned out to be the prettiest prom dress you ever looked at.

George put the top up on the car, and we all got in. When we got to the prom, I was feeling all self-conscious about my table cloth dress.

Some of the girls in the stag-ette line came up to me and started commenting on my dress.

"Sadie, your dress is beautiful."

"Sadie, that dress is slenderizing."

"Sadie, where did you get that beautiful dress? I've never seen another one like it."

"Sears and Roebuck," I lied. "It's in the new book."

George asked Mary Grace to dance first, and then he danced with Christina.

A fast dance started and George asked me to dance. George could really cut a rug on the dance floor. Everybody just stood back and watched as George and I danced, while the band played, "Good Golly, Miss Molly, sure like to dance."

Dusty walked in with Cherry, but nobody paid any attention to them.

After *"Good Golly, Miss Molly"* ended, George went up to Dusty. "You owe these girls an apology."

Dusty had never apologized to anyone in his life, but he apologized to us. He was a little afraid of George. George had a reputation for not putting up with crap, and he was six feet, six inches tall.

The next day, Frankie called Mary Grace. He said he was sorry for standing her up. He said he had never been on a date before, and he got nervous. That was fine with Mary Grace—she didn't want to go out with Frankie in the first place.

Now, I've got two bits of advice to everybody. First, if a pretty boy asks you out, run for your life. Nice pretty boys are few and far between. Second, if things don't go your way, make do with what you've got.

I never did Dusty's homework for him again, and he almost failed his senior year of high school.

Chapter 15

Senior Trip

When we started our senior year in high school, at the beginning of September, we went to work. We sold magazines, we baby sat, we took in ironing, we had bake sales, we had car washes, we sold candy, and we did yard work—anything to earn money for our senior class trip.

When those two big Greyhound busses pulled up in front of Pea Ridge High School, we were ready! Our mamas had worked for a year getting our wardrobes in shape for the trip. Mary Grace's mama would buy the cloth, and Christina's mama and Mama would make the clothes. We wore "triplet clothes" all of the time. Our wardrobe was beautiful.

Before we left the school, Christina wanted to ride on the bus with the "goody two-shoes". Mary Grace and I wanted to ride the "wild" bus. We won. Miss Anna and Miss Lucy rode the fun bus.

Before we were even out of Pea Ridge, some of the wild boys were passing around paper bags with bottles of Jack Daniels and moonshine in them. We were good girls, so we didn't partake.

Frankie Douglas got pretty looped, and he became very outgoing. Then, he started crying, "Mary Grace, Mary Grace, I can't believe I stood you up. You're the prettiest girl in Pea Ridge. I think I love you. Please go out with me. You can drive my car," he wailed.

"Here, eat some of this Spam sandwich—maybe it'll help to sober you up," I said.

"I'm going to smack you sober," Mary Grace said to Frankie.

About 2:00 A. M. everybody on the bus had either passed out or had fallen asleep. I woke up to find something strange in my mouth. It was a cigarette. Bully had put it there, and then he took a picture of me with the cigarette in my mouth. He threatened to send the picture of me to Mama. I guess he was still a little mad at me because I had called him "ugly".

That was not the only cigarette I smoked on the senior trip. We went to a pizza pie restaurant, and I shared a slice of pizza with Christina and Mary Grace. It tasted strange to our palette, and we didn't like it. We thought it smelled awful and tasted worse.

After we got the pizza down, Mary Grace, and I lit up cigarettes. We thought we would look very glamorous and grown up. Christina wouldn't even take one puff, and when Mary Grace and I inhaled our first drag, we started wheezing and coughing. We looked anything but glamorous—just a couple of country bumpkins gasping for breath with tears running down our faces.

Everybody in the restaurant knew it was our first cigarette. I prayed very hard to Jesus that no one would tell my mama!

The next morning, Moses Don Little put Pea Ridge on the map when he pulled out his Jew's harp and started playing on the street in New York City. People gathered around him to listen. I guess those Yankees didn't know what a Jew's harp was.

When we got into the hotel and got checked in, the girls were on the eighteenth floor, and the boys were right under us on the seventeenth floor. The boys who were directly under us, especially Wallace, were cute. They stuck their heads out of the window and yelled up to us.

We chatted back and forth for a few minutes, and then I came up with the idea to pour a little water down on them. We did this several times. I guess you could say that we were a bit immature.

The boys would stick their heads out of the window, and we would try to hit them in the head with water from a glass that we found in the bathroom. They would jerk their heads back in the window so they wouldn't get hit, and they were winning. Not a drop of water hit them.

Then, I decided that more water was needed, and this is the part where the terrible trouble started. I got an entire pitcher of water and dumped it all at once. Just as I dumped it, a woman walked out of the hotel bar onto the sidewalk. That poor woman got soaked from head to toe. She was not happy one bit, and she called the police. I was scared to death!

The police came up, and I met them in the hall. "I did it. I did it," I confessed, my hands held up over my head. "Please don't call my mama. I'm so sorry," I cried.

The police gave me a lecture, and then they went to Miss Lucy and told her what had happened. Miss Lucy told me how disappointed she was in me. She said that since this was the first time for me to be in trouble that she would let it go, but for me to be on my best behavior for the rest of this trip.

I promised her that I would.

Chapter 16

Poor Triplets, Up a Creek without a Paddle

We got dressed in our very best outfits: white Orlon blouse, black straight skirt with a kick pleat up the back, and black six inch heels.

The Class of 1961, Pea Ridge High School, was going to Radio City Music Hall in New York City to see the Rockettes. This was the highlight of our senior trip.

Mary Grace, Christina, and I were the last ones out of the hotel because Mary Grace couldn't get her bee hive just right. We were running for our bus when Christina got the heel of her shoe caught in a crack in the sidewalk. We were screaming for the bus driver to wait for us, but he was too far away to hear us. That Greyhound just drove right off and left us. Christina struggled with the shoe, and finally the heel of her pump broke off in the crack of the sidewalk.

We couldn't miss Radio City Music Hall and the Rockettes, so we decided that we could get there on our own. We had never hailed a cab before, but we started waving our arms in the air, and a taxi pulled over ahead of us. We started trotting toward the cab, and a woman passed us like we were standing still. She got in the cab, and it took off, leaving us with our mouths hanging open.

We had some choices—try to hail another cab, go back to the hotel, or take the subway. We took the subway.

We hopped on the crowded subway car. We thought we could ask the driver where to get off, but there was no driver. We asked several people, but they completely ignored us. We debated about what we should do.

We thought we ought to get off at Central Park. We knew our hotel overlooked Central Park, but we didn't know how big Central Park is.

Then, we saw three girls who looked a lot like us.

"Can you tell us where the Plaza Hotel is?" asked Mary Grace.

We weren't staying at the Plaza Hotel, but our hotel was close by.

The girls were very evil. They laughed at us. "Listen to the hicks," said girl number one. "I think they're lost."

"I'll bet they've got money," said girl number two.

We had combined all of our money, our hotel room key, and identification in one purse, which Mary Grace was carrying.

Girl number three ran up behind Mary Grace and pushed her hard. Mary Grace fell down.

Girl number one grabbed our communal purse and threw it to girl number two. The three girls took off, running as fast as they could.

We chased them, but to no avail. We found out later that they were juvenile delinquents who stole purses to support themselves.

We sat down on a park bench. Christina was hysterical.

"What are we going to do? Oh, what are we going to do," Christina sobbed. She was wringing her hands, and mascara was running down her face.

We sat on the bench and watched people walk by, trying to find a kind face. We had never seen such people in our lives.

We had no idea what to do. We were hungry, and the sun was going down.

We spotted a mounted policeman. Before we could say a word, the policeman started shouting, "I've been looking for you, you robbers. I let you loose one time, and I won't again!"

"We're not them," Christina shouted.

"That's what you said the last time," said the policeman.

"We're from Pea Ridge, Tennessee," I shouted back.

"Run," shouted Mary Grace.

We all ran in a different direction. This confused the horse, and he started going around in circles.

Now we were separated. I cried out, "Mary Grace ... Christina ... where are you?"

"Over here," Mary Grace whispered back, hiding behind a tree.

We walked through the park, yelling for Christina. We finally found her, huddled in the corner of a public restroom. She had a cup of stale, half-eaten popcorn in her hand.

"Lord Jesus, I'm going to be good for the rest of my life," prayed Christina. "If You will just get me back to Pea Ridge, I'll never leave there again."

"Christina, you *are* good," said Mary Grace.

"What are we going to do?" I was near hysterics myself.

We got up and looked at ourselves in the cracked mirror. We looked just like the other people in the park. Christina's face was black with mascara, and she walked with a limp because her pump heel was broken off. Mary Grace's hair was a mess. The kick pleat of her skirt was torn all the way to her waist band, and she was dirty. I had scratched my arms when I was running from the policeman—I had run into a rose bush, and blood was all over my face and clothes. Our stockings were in tatters.

We left the restroom and started walking. As we started to walk, it began to rain. If ever I wanted to die, it was then.

We ate the stale popcorn, and for some reason, Christina kept the cup.

In the distance we saw a light. When we came closer, we saw it was a restaurant, made out of glass and mirrors. The sign overhead said, "Tavern on the Green".

"Are we in heaven?" asked Christina.

"No," I said. "It's a restaurant, I think."

When we walked in the restaurant, a hush fell over the entire place.

"Please, please help us," I said.

A man in a black suit—bigger, even, than George Washington Green, escorted us out of the place.

"Go around to the back," he said. "I'll bring you something to eat."

We realized that he thought we were homeless beggars, but he brought us some of the best food we had ever tasted.

"Now get outa here," he said, "before I call the police."

We started walking again. Now, we were broke, pitiful, raggedy, and scared to death.

"Please, please help us," we begged every person we saw.

Most people ignored us. Some kept on talking among themselves. Some scorned us, saying, "You got what you deserve." I guess they had never been robbed by bandit bad girls.

Some people looked at us with pity, and then turned away. We kept on pleading, "Please, please somebody, we need help."

A couple of people of foreign descent thought we were beggars. They put money in Christina's popcorn cup, and then, others started doing the same thing.

We were feeling a little better. We now had a cup full of change. Now, at least, we could get back to the hotel.

Then, out of nowhere, came the same policeman on horseback.

"I've got you now," he shouted. "Put your hands in the air! Panhandling is against the law! You're going to reform school!"

We didn't even try to run. Reform school had to be better than this mess we're in, I thought to myself.

Then, another policeman galloped up on his mount.

"I've got 'em," Dobbins said.

"Let's question them," said the other policeman, Preston. "It could be a case of mistaken identity. There's a *bolo* (be on the lookout) for three girls from Tennessee. They're missing from a high school senior trip. We've been looking for them all afternoon."

"That's us! That's us!" we all shouted at the same time.

"They got those juvie girls earlier this afternoon," said Preston. "They're down at the precinct right now, but they fit the description of these girls. Dobbins, you hold these girls here, and I'll go get a car. I'll take these girls back to the precinct. The teacher and the principal are there—maybe they can identify these three."

Preston came back with a police car, and we all got in and drove down to the precinct house. Miss Anna and Miss Lucy met us at the door. They didn't look much better than we did.

After we got through crying and hugging each other, Miss Anna said, "What on earth happened? When we got to Radio City Music Hall, we realized you weren't with us, and we came back to get you, but you weren't there."

We told them the whole story.

"Mary Grace," Miss Lucy said, "we got your purse back. The three girls who got arrested were trying to pass themselves off as you, Christina, and Sadie. They went to the hotel to use your key to get in your room. We just happened to be standing near them, and we called the police to tell them they were impostors."

Things were looking up, but we had missed Radio City Music Hall and the Rockettes.

"Miss Anna, after all the trouble we have caused, I hate to even mention this, but we really wanted to see the Rockettes, bad," said Christina.

"Well," Miss Anna said, "we're certainly glad you're alright, and we're glad we found you, but we missed the Rockettes, too."

"I have an idea," said Preston, who was impressed with Mary Grace's radiant good looks. "I'm off duty, and I can take all of you tonight."

"But we can't leave a bus load of wild teenagers alone in New York City," said Miss Lucy.

"Well, let me check with the chief and Dobbins. Maybe Dobbins and another officer can be in charge of the wild kids. It might do them some good."

"Sounds like a plan," said Miss Lucy.

That night we got dressed in our second prettiest matching outfits and Preston took us to see the Rockettes. They were awesome!

Life was good again.

Chapter 17

High School Graduation

A week before the seniors of 1961 were to graduate, Alice Ivy Green came home from college for the weekend. Alice Ivy had graduated from high school the year before us.

She had waited a long time to get even with Emma Jean Hollowell, the home economics teacher, for making her pick out stitches in her apron and baking a pie, which Emma Jean entered in a contest.

Alice Ivy and George Washington came by and picked up Mary Grace, Christina, and me. We drove past Emma Jean's house five or six times.

Emma Jean had washed clothes, and she was hanging out her big old drawers.

"Let's wait until she's not at home, and then we'll carry out my plan," said Alice Ivy.

"Let's go to the Dairy Dip and get banana splits," said Mary Grace.

Mary Grace could eat a cow and never gain an ounce.

When we got to the Dairy Dip, Mary Grace got her banana split, and the rest of us got small ice cream cones.

"What's the plan?" asked George.

Alice Ivy replied, "We'll wait until Emma Jean leaves her house. This is Saturday, and she goes grocery shopping on Saturdays. When she's gone, we'll steal a pair of her big old drawers."

"Let's drive by her house again," said George, "and see if she's gone to the store yet."

George was mad at Emma Jean, too, because she wouldn't let him take Home Ec. Emma Jean was very mean spirited. She had told George that men had no business in the kitchen—that cooking was woman's work, and he was a sissy if he wanted to learn to cook.

Second to doctoring, cooking was George's favorite thing to do.

When we got to Emma Jean's house, we were in luck. Emma Jean had gone to the store, and there was nobody around to witness our crime.

Alice Ivy got out of the car and ran up to the clothes line. She grabbed a pair of Emma Jean's extra-extra large drawers. They were red, with "Emma Jean" embroidered in blue across the butt.

Alice Ivy jumped in the car, and we kicked up dust getting out of there.

We laughed our heads off at the thought of Emma Jean Hollowell in those drawers.

I wanted to get even with Buford Posey, the football coach. I had Coach Posey for P. E. during my senior year, and I couldn't make any higher than a C+ in his class, no matter how hard I tried. I could have graduated at least fifth in my class, if it wasn't for that P. E. grade.

As it stood, Mary Grace was the class valedictorian, and Christina was the class salutatorian. I ranked tenth in our class of 100.

I told Alice Ivy how mad I was at Buford Posey.

"Well," she said, "get even with him." Alice Ivy had no problem with getting even, and making things right was her specialty.

"How?" I asked.

"I'll come up with something good. Just give me a while," said Alice Ivy.

"Come by the house tomorrow," said George. "We'll have a plan by then."

I absolutely loved George. He was very nice to me, but I think he only liked me as a friend. I wanted to spend the rest of my life with him.

The next day, after church, we went to Alice Ivy's and George's house. Alice Ivy met us at the door.

"I've got it," she said. "Come on in, and we'll tell you all about it. It's perfect!"

George was in the kitchen cooking chicken and dumplings.

"Here's the plan," he said. "Tell everybody in your class to bring a roll of loosely wrapped pennies to graduation. Coach Posey'll be helping to hand out diplomas. When he gives them their diploma, they hand him the roll of pennies."

We were so excited about graduating from high school. All three of us were going to college. Christina, and I knew we were going to be teachers. (I wanted to be just like Miss Anna.) Mary Grace was not exactly happy with her three choices—teacher, nurse, or secretary.

We were good girls, smart and confident. We had the world by the tail! But, before we faced the world, we had to raise a little hell.

Three days before graduation, Mary Grace and I told everybody in our class about the pennies. A few of the "holy roller" students objected—they thought it might be a sin to do that to Coach Posey.

We explained to them that it was their Christian duty. Coach Posey would wind up with a total of $50.00, so actually, they would be a part of giving him a very large gift. Fifty dollars was a lot of money in those days.

The big day finally came. We were grownups, now. A few of us would go to college in the fall, but most would get married or get a job.

Mary Grace and Christina had spent the night with me the night before graduation day so we could get a ride to school with Bully and not have to take the school bus.

The first thing we saw when we got to school was Emma Jean Hollowell's big old drawers flapping in the wind. George and Alice Ivy had run them up the flag pole.

There was no doubt in anybody's mind as to who those big drawers belonged to.

When Emma Jean got to school and saw her drawers at the top of the flag pole, she threw such a hissy fit that you could hear her screaming a mile away.

She accused Dusty of doing it. She said she was going to call the sheriff and have Dusty arrested. She said she was going to quit teaching, but she took that back real quick because she knew Miss Lucy would be glad to see her go.

Miss Anna called Dr. Pooten. He came right over to the school and gave Emma Jean a shot to calm her down. He told her to go on back home and go to bed.

Mary Grace and Christina both gave speeches that night, and I sat in seat number ten.

Coach Posey was absolutely delighted when the first twenty seniors gave him the loosely rolled pennies. After thirty seniors had passed him, Coach Posey's pants were sagging around his hips. After thirty-five seniors, Coach Posey tightened his belt. After forty seniors, he started to put the pennies in his jacket pocket. After fifty seniors, he tightened his belt again. His hips and chest were getting quite large.

Coach Posey filled every pocket to its capacity, and then he started pushing the rolls down in his pants pockets. The pennies were loosely rolled, so this made the coins come out of their wrappers.

As he handed senior number sixty his diploma, Coach Posey's belt broke and his pants fell to the floor. Pennies flew everywhere!

Coach Posey turned around to try to pick up some of the loose coins. When he did, we couldn't believe what we saw! Coach Posey's drawers were red, with "Buford" embroidered in blue across his butt.

We all knew, then, that the rumors that we had been hearing about Coach Posey and Emma Jean were true. They surely deserved each other. There was only one problem about this relationship—Coach Posey was married.

Coach Posey was a high tempered fool, so needless to say, he was not happy about the whole situation.

He grabbed senior number sixty-one, who happened to be Willie Westley, around the neck and started to choke him. Poor little Willie was scared to death.

"You bastards! I'm going to fail every one of you," he ranted. His face was blood red, and he was foaming at the mouth.

Our principal, Miss Lucy, had wanted to fire Coach Posey for years. Here was her chance.

"Coach Posey," she yelled, "take your hands off little Willie. Get your belongings out of the gym and don't come back next year."

"You're firing me, you uppity bitch?" he hollered as he grabbed for Lucy's neck.

That was not a good idea. Dignity was thrown to the wind. Miss Anna and Miss Lucy wrestled Coach Posey to the floor and sat on him.

Hoss was a burly young man who was manager of the fresh meat department at the Piggly Wiggly, and he was very protective of Miss Anna and Miss Lucy. He came to all of the school functions to make sure that Miss Anna and Miss Lucy were safe. He always stood at the back of the auditorium, by the door.

When the ruckus started, Hoss ran to the stage and got Coach Posey in a head lock. Hoss dragged Coach Posey up the aisle, out of the back door, tied him up with a rope, and put him on the back of his pickup truck. Hoss drove Coach Posey straight to jail.

Miss Anna and Miss Lucy got up off of the floor of the stage, patted their hair, straightened their clothes, and continued to pass out the diplomas. Miss Betty Sue, the typing teacher, got a bucket out of the janitor's closet and instructed the graduates to deposit their pennies in it.

Miss Anna suspected that it was George and Alice Ivy who were somehow involved in this escapade, but she never said a word to them about it.

Nobody ever suspected Mary Grace or Christina or me, either.

We were new at the "getting even" game, but we sure liked it.

Chapter 18

The Original Big Hair Girls

The original big hair girls were "raised right". We were pure, kind, generous, God-fearing, and incredibly naive. This made us walking targets for bullies and scoundrels. We were a reflection of our mamas, and they made sure that we made them proud.

We were polite at all costs. Once, Mama's Aunt Dot, who was ninety years old, made me a dress out of a feed sack. It had the words, "Purina Cow Feed" right across my butt. Mama made me wear it to Aunt Dot's house. She said that if I didn't wear it, it would hurt Aunt Dot's feelings.

It was so embarrassing that I thought I might die!

The fact that I wore the dress encouraged Aunt Dot, and she made me "pretty little dresses" until the day she died.

In the 1980's, feed-sack dresses were a fad. I bought one, but I never got the courage to wear it in public. I gave it to the Good Will store with the $50.00 price tag still on it.

It was the job of the "raised right" girls to make sure that boys didn't ruin us. Often, this wasn't easy.

I knew I wanted to marry George, but he hadn't asked me out on a date, yet. I was with him a lot, but it was always with a group of friends.

I wasn't one to sit home and wait for anyone. I dated lots of boys—boring boys, dumb boys, and a few ugly boys if they were smart. Occasionally, I dated one that I liked.

Usually, I dumped them or they dumped me, after we had had three dates. It seemed to me that the wild girls had more fun than the "raised right" girls.

The trashy girls got a raw deal all the way around. Boys would not want to be seen with them. These girls didn't have any friends, because the "raised right" girls' mamas wouldn't let us talk to them.

The boys spread rumors about them. They had "raised right" girl friends who they took to church and home to their mamas, and they had a trashy girl on the side.

The wild girls were different from the trashy girls. The wild girls were very popular, and most often had rich daddies. All the boys wanted to go out with the wild girls. The wild girls would drink, smoke, and lead the boys on.

I was a "raised right" good girl—but I did let boys kiss me, after the third date.

One reason that I was so good was, every time we passed a cemetery, my Mama would say, "Sadie Rose, I would rather see you dead and lying in a grave over there than to see you ruin yourself." (Mama, I would think, you can't ruin yourself—you have to have some help). That statement gave me the incentive to stay as pure as the new fallen snow.

The boys could get quite creative in trying to persuade the "raised right" girls to "go all the way". Here are a few of the favorites:

"I love you so much, if I can't have you, I'm going to kill myself."

"I'm going in the army, and I may never see you again."

"I'm going to marry you when I get the money."

"I love you more than anybody else on earth."

"I would die for you."

Most of the time, the "raised right" big hair girls would not be persuaded, but occasionally, a "raised right" girl would be overcome with passion.

Once, Esther came into the dorm after being out on a date with Dewey. They were "in love" and they had been going steady for two years. When she started to the shower, we noticed that her step-ins were on backwards and inside out. We knew for sure that she was ruined, and she was going to hell.

Another time, Christina came back to the dorm after being on a double date. She was pale and shaking like a leaf.

"What on earth happened?" asked Mary Grace.

"I think Gloria and Geeter 'did it' in the back seat," she said. "The car was shaking and the back window fogged up!"

Gloria didn't exactly fall into any particular category. She was from a very prominent family, and she was sort of wild, but it was hard for her to get dates because she was 6' 2" tall.

"Raised right" girls had other choices to make, in addition to not ruining themselves. A "raised right" girl could make her life easier if she was very smart, but she pretended that she wasn't. Or she could be very pleasant. I chose pleasant because it was easier than pretending.

Chapter 19

Look Everybody, Sadie Rose is Here

I had been a freshman for exactly two days when the "big fall" occurred. I was both excited and nervous about being a college girl.

I was dressed in my gathered skirt, sleeveless blouse, and Queen Ann shoes. It was 10:00 A. M. and everybody on campus was out of class. Mary Grace and I had been to the campus book store to buy our books for the semester. I was so loaded down with books, notebooks, and other supplies that I could barely see over the top of them.

We were walking down the steps of the administration building. We were ten steps from the bottom when an awful thing happened—I turned my ankle over, and I lost my balance.

I tumbled the rest of the way down the steps. Books, notebooks, and supplies went flying everywhere, and a huge crowd of students gathered around me. My skirt flew over my head, and my panties were showing. I was in terrible pain.

What was I going to do? Pretend I was dead? Cry? This was so, so humiliating. I did the only thing a self-respecting college girl could do—I got up off the ground, and I took a bow!

Everybody in the crowd gave me a big round of applause and helped me gather my belongings.

Mary Grace and I went on to our next class. When I sat down in my desk, I looked down at my knee. It was the size of a small cantaloupe.

I waited, and I suffered in silence until I got back to my dorm room, and then I bawled. A little while later, George Washington called me.

"Sadie Rose," he said, "I heard about your fall."

"Well, just go ahead and laugh," I screamed.

"No, Sadie Rose, I'm not laughing. I've been to the drug store and I bought an Ace bandage. I'm coming over to give you medical assistance, if that's alright with you."

"George, I lo …", and then I stopped. I almost told him that I loved him.

"I'd appreciate that very much," I said.

George came right over and gently bandaged my swollen knee.

"Sadie Rose," he said, "take two aspirin and go to bed."

"George, I for sure don't ever want to be a wall flower, but this was just an awful way to get attention."

"Sadie Rose, you don't ever have to worry about being a wall flower. Everybody likes you. You're pretty, you're smart, and you're sweet."

I was praying so hard, "Please, please, add 'and I love you, sweet Sadie'", but he didn't.

All I could blubber out was, "Thanks, George."

Chapter 20

Green Freshman

Mary Grace, Christina, and I were so excited. We were turned loose on the world.

I thought college would be like high school. Wrong! Wrong! Wrong!

In high school, all three of us were at the top of our graduating class. College was different. College was hard. College professors didn't cut you any slack. When I got my first semester grades back, I thought I would either die or that my mama would kill me.

The three of us were roommates. We had to be in charge of ourselves. Nobody asked us if our homework was done, nor did they care.

Freshman students could not have cars on campus. Every night we would walk down Main Street to our favorite restaurant. Main Street was lined with beautiful mansions.

"I want that one," said Mary Grace.

"I want that one," said Christina.

"I want that one," I said.

We would pick the houses we wanted to live in. Rich people lived in those houses, and we dreamed of being rich.

Mary Grace and I dated a lot. We could go out any time we wanted to. We didn't even have to ask.

Dating came in real handy. We would never eat before we went on a date.

"What do you want to do?" our date would ask.

"Go out to eat," we would always answer.

Those boys contributed to our college education.

When we didn't have a date to feed us, we went to Boot's Restaurant.

Boot's had the best food I have ever eaten in my life: country fried steak, mashed potatoes and gravy, green beans, corn pone, and biscuits.

Mrs. Boot was the meanest woman alive. She was a very heavy set woman, and she would sit on a bar stool and frown down at us.

Mrs. Boot's butt hung off all the way around that bar stool. She frowned down on us, even when we were on our best behavior, but mostly, we were not even on good behavior. We would cut up and giggle all the time. It's a wonder we didn't give that poor old thing a heart attack.

Being in charge of myself was not an easy task.

First of all, there was the money management. I got $10.00 a week allowance. This had to buy my food, clothing, and entertainment. There was no such thing as, "I'll call Daddy," or, "I'll put it on my credit card".

Then, there was the laundry. I either had to wash my clothes occasionally or just wear dirty clothes.

Even more important, there was the matter of my hair.

Chapter 21

How to Have Big Hair

Big hair is my favorite kind of hair.

First of all, it balances out your head with your body, unless you are really skinny. If you are really skinny, then your head looks too big for your body. If you're on the pudgy side, big hair is perfect hair.

The privileged girls went to the beauty shop once a week and got their hair washed, teased, lacquered, and sprayed. Mary Grace, Christina, and I did our own hair.

Doing our own hair was a long process. First we washed our hair. Then, we put Dippity-Doo on our wet head. After this, we rolled it on orange juice cans, put a hair net on, and went to bed.

I don't think I had a good night's sleep during the entire four years I was at college.

The next morning, we would get up and tease our hair, and I don't mean just a little, either. Then, we brushed the top layer over the tangled mess. We put it in a flip, a French twist, or a bee hive. The last thing we did was to spray it with lacquer. That hair would not move for a whole week! If your head itched, you had to scratch it with a pencil.

Mary Grace, Christina, and I shared everything, including lacquer. Once, we all ran out of lacquer at once, so we made a concoction of sugar and water that we sprayed on our hair. It worked just fine until we stood next to a honeysuckle bush where bees were buzzing around. Those bees got a whiff of our sugar-coated hair, and they went into a buzzing frenzy.

We were flinging our arms, trying to fight off the bees. One of them somehow got in my coiffure and stung me on the head.

We ran back to our dorm room and washed our sugar-coated hair. We had to wear flat hair and a head scarf until we had enough money to buy a bottle of lacquer.

When we had a special occasion that arose, Esther would fix our hair. Esther could make us look just like a movie star.

Chapter 22

God Takes Care of College Girls and Fools—The Wreck

At this point in my life, I fit into both categories—I was a college girl, but I was also a big fool.

I loved my '57 Chevy Impala hardtop more than anything. That car would fly, and I loved flying.

I would get my friends from the dorm in the car, and we would slip off and drive back to Pea Ridge.

I loved to bring my friends home to visit Mama. I loved my Impala, but I loved Mama even more. Mama would feed us, give us advice, and keep us laughing. We would visit with Mama for awhile, and then we would have to get back to the dorm.

One Thursday afternoon we had slipped off to Pea Ridge, and we had to get back before supper. We all had assigned seats in the dining hall, and they would know it if we weren't there.

We got in the car, and I "put the pedal to the metal". On the way back to college, we were laughing and carrying on. We came up behind a National Guard truck full of good looking soldiers in the back. We passed them like they were sitting still. We honked and waved.

"Eat my dust," I yelled.

A misty rain started to gently fall, but I didn't slow down. I turned on the windshield wipers and kept on truckin'.

Then, an awful thing happened. A dog in heat, and her boyfriend, ran out in front of us. I slammed on the brakes, but the car didn't slow down. There must have been oil on the road, because the car started to spin around and around in the road. I lost control of the car, and it went off the road onto the shoulder and through a picket fence.

Pickets were flying everywhere, including inside the car. We were screaming and dodging fence posts. Thank you, God, for saving our lives.

When the car finally stopped, I asked, "Mary Grace, are you alright?"

"Yes."

"Christina, how about you?"

"I'm O. K."

"Alice Ivy, are you alright?"

"Yes."

"Esther, are you O. K.?"

"Yes, I'm still here."

There wasn't a scratch on any of us. However, I had a very large bruise on my butt.

"Oh, my car, my beautiful car," I cried.

That car was totaled!

We had all of the side windows rolled up—to keep our bouffant hair in place. When the car stopped, we had no side windows to roll up or down. Every window in that car was broken out. The windshield was lying in shards on the dashboard. Glass was everywhere—in our hair and in our mouths.

The National Guard truck caught up with us about that time. They could see what the situation was, and they offered to take everybody back to the dorm.

Alice Ivy, Esther, and Christina piled in the front seat of the truck.

Even though we didn't have a windshield and the front axle was a little bent, the Impala was drivable. Mary Grace and I drove back to Pea Ridge, with me fighting to keep the car from going off on the shoulder of the road all the way back home.

We had to stop and get air in all of the tires. Every tire was going flat.

We finally got the car to the shop where Bully worked. We parked in the shop's parking lot, and Bully took us back to the dorm.

Mrs. Raddle, our dorm mother, was happy that we came back to the dorm safely, but she "campused" us for two weeks. We could only go to classes or stay in our dorm room.

Mrs. Raddle had finally caught the Songbird Girls doing what she suspected we had been doing all fall—slipping off campus. She was absolutely delighted that she had caught us, and she smiled and hummed for a solid month.

Chapter 23

Do You Know the Way to Detroit?

After our big wreck, we had to have wheels again.

Jo Lee's daddy owned an auto mechanic's shop in Michigan. He said that he would be glad to find me a new car.

Mama said that I could go to Michigan, but I had to pay for the trip myself.

Mary Grace and I did a lot of planning. Mary Grace had friends and relatives in Chicago. We wanted to go to Chicago first, and then to Detroit, but Mama said "No".

Mary Grace didn't even ask her parents. We just boarded that big old Greyhound, disobeyed our parents, and slipped off.

Greyhound gets you where you're going, but it's a hard ride. Within an hour of getting on that bus, I knew we were in trouble.

First of all, I had to go to the bathroom. Second of all, we were hungry. And third of all, the bus didn't go the shortest way to Chicago. We went through every little Podunk town, and we stopped at every one of them, but we weren't allowed to get off the bus. We found that out the hard way.

The second stop we made was Bowling Green, Kentucky. Mary Grace and I got off the bus to go to the bathroom, and that big old Greyhound just drove right off and left us. Our luggage was on the bus!

We had to wait for three hours for the next bus to Chicago. We got on the second bus and we encountered a weirdo.

He sat right across the aisle from us on the bus. When we stopped for our lunch and bathroom break in Fairfield, Illinois, we had a half-hour. The food was awful and the bathroom was nasty, but the worst thing was our weirdo. He sat at the table next to ours, and he didn't say a word—he just stared at us.

When we came out of the bathroom, he was standing right in front of the ladies room door, staring and waiting for us.

He was so creepy, and we were scared.

When we stopped in Tuscola, he followed the same routine. He did not take his eyes off of us. He stood outside the bathroom door and waited for us to come out.

By this time, we were really tired. My feet were swollen, and we were not willing to put up with much more weird behavior.

When we came out of the bathroom, Mary Grace said, "Please quit looking at us."

"Don't follow us anymore," I said.

"It's a free country," the weirdo said. "I can look anywhere I want to look, at whoever I want to look at, and you or nobody else can stop me."

Alice Ivy Green had talked to us before we left, and we knew exactly what to do. Mary Grace grabbed his arms, and I kicked him-hard-between his legs.

We both ran as fast as we could and got back on the bus.

The weirdo was bent over in pain when our bus pulled out of the station. The rest of the trip was still tiring, but much more pleasant.

When we got to the Greyhound station in Chicago, we tried to retrieve our suitcases. The station manager made some telephone calls and told us that our luggage would be in Chicago in about a week. "But, we're supposed to be in Detroit by then," we wailed.

The station manager took the telephone number of Mary Grace's friend and told us that just as soon as the suitcases came in, he would give us a call.

Robbie, Mary Grace's friend, came to the bus station to pick us up. She took us to her house in Olive Park, right on the shore of Lake Michigan.

The next day we went across town to Joliet, one of Chicago's suburbs. Robbie worked at the Midwest Amusement Park there. This was her off day, and she got us in for half price.

Mary Grace, Robbie, and I got in the barrel ride. It's the ride where you stand against the wall of the barrel, and it starts to spin around. As it spins faster, the bottom drops out of the barrel, and centrifugal force keeps you on the side of the barrel. Well, when the barrel started to slow down, my foot caught in the bottom. I lost my balance and fell down. I tumbled around and around and around, and *that* was no fun at all!

When we left the amusement park, Robbie took us for a ride around the loop on the el—the elevated train. I had never seen anything like that!

The next day we went back to the Greyhound station to get on the bus for Detroit. The station manager said that as soon as he found our bags, he would send them on to Jo Lee's house in Detroit.

We got to Detroit without any more trouble with weirdoes. We were just dead tired.

Jo Lee's parents picked us up at the bus station. After we told the station manager there about our luggage situation, he took Jo Lee's telephone number and said he would call us when the suitcases finally showed up.

Chapter 24

The Songbird Girls Ride Again

I had written Jo Lee a letter every day for two weeks before our trip. I was so happy to see her again when we finally got to Michigan. We were crying and laughing and jumping up and down.

Jo Lee had lots of plans for us. First of all, she got her boyfriend to get us dates. I think maybe she should have given him a little more time to get us acquainted with these fellows.

When we were introduced to them, Mary Grace quickly chose the beatnik. He was almost handsome—tall and dark, with a moustache and goatee. Jo Lee's date was drop-dead gorgeous. He looked like Fabian.

I've already given you my opinion of pretty boys. My date was an albino. His eyes were pink, and he was shorter than me, and he was absolutely the nicest boy (excluding George) that I had ever met. Of course, at that time, George didn't know I was in love with him.

Pinkie was his nickname, and I could have had a long-term relationship with him if we had lived closer to each other.

The boys took us out to eat, and then we went to a séance. I had never heard of a séance. When it started, the only light in the room was a single candle sitting on a low coffee table. We sat on the floor around it.

On the coffee table was an Ouija board. When the séance started, weird and creepy things went on.

The way the Ouija board works is, you ask the board questions, and a pointer that you gently touch with your fingertips would spell out the answers. You could feel your fingers being moved by some sort of mysterious power, and you couldn't feel that power if you weren't touching the pointer.

I really hoped that Brother Wright would never find out about our séance. He would say that we were playing with Satan, and that was a sin, and we were all going to Hell.

The beatnik beat on his bongo drum and everybody chanted.

Then, they brought out the marijuana and rolled it into cigarettes. Mary Grace and I had only smoked one Lucky Strike in our whole lives, and Jo Lee didn't smoke either. We didn't know anybody who smoked marijuana, and we weren't about to smoke "wacky-weed".

I told Pinkie that we had to leave, even if we had to walk back to Jo Lee's house. Pinkie quickly said that he would drive us back. Neither he nor Jo Lee's boyfriend smoked marijuana.

When we drove off, Mary Grace's date was still sitting at the coffee table, beating his bongo drum and smoking marijuana.

Chapter 25

Back to Pea Ridge

The next day we went car shopping. Jo Lee's daddy, Miller, had us a very reliable car picked out. We wanted no part of that! We wanted a pretty car!

Miller went with us, and we shopped around until we found a beautiful '57 Ford Tudor convertible that was within my budget. This one was reliable, too, but it was much more expensive than the ugly car that Miller had picked out for us. I could afford the Tudor, barely, and so I bought it.

Our suitcases still hadn't come, so Trudy bought us some step-ins and some toothbrushes. We tried very hard to find something in Jo Lee's closet to wear, but it was no use. Nothing fit, and Trudy's clothes wouldn't fit, either.

Trudy took us on a trip to Frankenmuth, a German work community. The people there weren't like the people in Pea Ridge at all. They talked funny, but their chicken dinners sure were good!

Our clothes were getting pretty ripe by this time. Our suitcases were somewhere in America. Would we ever see them again?

Trudy had an idea. She took us to the Salvation Army store to get clothes. We took one look at those clothes and said that we would just wear our dirty clothes. All they had there was just a bunch of worn out house dresses.

We went back to Jo Lee's house and looked in every closet. Then, we got creative.

Mary Grace was very tall and slim. Jo Lee had a pair of pants that fit perfectly, except they were way too short. Mary Grace rolled up the legs and made her a pair of pedal pushers. I found a pair of shorts in Trudy's closet.

Next, we went to Miller's closet and got white shirts. We rolled up the sleeves, turned up the collars, put a scarf around our heads, and tied them in a bow on top of our heads. We were fashionable and happy.

The next day we got directions from Miller about how to get back to Pea Ridge. We put the top down and hauled ourselves back to Tennessee.

Neither of us had ever driven on an interstate highway before. We almost had another wreck when we merged into four-lane traffic without looking.

"What's wrong with you—you got your head up your ass?" shouted the woman who almost hit us. It seemed to me like people were always calling Mary Grace and me ugly names for no reason.

We drove until it was nearly dark. Then, we started looking for a motel that we could afford. We finally found a seedy looking one, but the rooms there were just $9.00 a night.

After we checked in and got in our room, we pushed the dresser in front of the door and slept with a shoe under the pillow.

The next day, we pulled into Pea Ridge with our top down, looking quite cute. I had exactly one dollar in my purse when we got in my driveway.

Chapter 26

Ain't You Had No Raising?

Muff Mosley, a Yankee girl who lived in our dorm, was absolutely obnoxious. She would do us ugly every time she got the chance.

She would borrow our clothes without asking, and when we would ask for them back, she would return them dirty. She would insult us and say, "Can't you afford ready-made clothes? These old home-made things are tacky."

Muff always objected to giving us gas fund money, and Mary Grace got tired of it.

"Let's drive off and leave her," said Mary Grace.

We did this several times, and Muff soon got the message—pay up or don't ride.

We couldn't stand that old Yankee girl. She would tell Miss Raddle on us.

"Sadie Rose Marie has been roller skating in the hall again," she would say, and I would get demerits for it. I had to save my demerits for a messy room—we always had a messy room.

One time, Muff wanted us to take her to her uncle's house to get some money. We reluctantly agreed. She put 25¢ in the peanut butter jar, and we started driving.

We drove and drove, and we were getting pretty far out into the country.

"I think we're lost," I said. "Personally, I can't find my way out of a paper bag."

"I thought you said that he lives in town," said Christina.

"I know the way," said Muff. "This is a short cut."

We stopped the car near a persimmon tree in somebody's yard. Muff stole persimmons and started eating them.

We took a bathroom break behind a tree, and then we started driving again. Muff ate persimmons and started bossing us around.

"You'd better not eat any more of those persimmons," said Christina.

Muff told Christina to shut up.

Well, about ten miles down the road, Muff asked Mary Grace to stop the car. She grabbed my handkerchief that Grandma Rose Lena had given me. It had hand woven lace around the edges, and I usually saved it for Sunday.

Muff ran behind some bushes to use the bathroom. When she returned, she didn't have my handkerchief with her.

"Where's my handkerchief?" I asked.

"Behind the bushes. Where did you think it is?" asked Muff.

I cried for a little while about the handkerchief, and then I got really mad. We kept on driving.

Ten more miles down the road, Muff cried out, "Stop the car! I've got to go again!"

"We told you not to eat all those persimmons," said Christina.

"I need some toilet paper," said Muff.

"Where do you think we are," asked Mary Grace, "at the grocery store? You'll just have to use a leaf."

"That's barbaric! I'm not using a leaf," said Muff.

"You're not getting *my* handkerchief," said Mary Grace.

Muff was in a fix, so she just took off running through the woods. In a few minutes she came back.

We said that we were turning around and going back to the dorm. Muff threw another fit about that.

We didn't care. We'd had enough.

We started trying to find our way back to the dorm. After a while, Muff started to scratch. Big blisters started to show up on her hands. Then, she started to scratch her rear end.

"What kind of leaf did you use?" asked Christina.

"A whole bunch of little leaves growing up a tree," said Muff.

"You're supposed to use a poke salad leaf, or an oak leaf," said Christina. "I'm afraid you got a hold of some poison ivy."

"You bunch of country hicks! Whoever heard of substituting leaves for toilet paper, anyway? I hate all of you," Muff screamed.

"We'd better take you to Dr. Pooten," said Christina.

Christina was, by far, the kindest and sweetest of the three of us. Mary Grace and I thought that Muff got what she deserved. After all, poison ivy won't kill you ... unless you happen to call Alice Ivy Green "poison ivy". She scared the crap out of Nobel one time, when he called her "poison ivy".

We finally found our way back to Pea Ridge and took Muff to the hospital.

Dr. Pooten was flabbergasted. "How on earth did you get poison ivy on that area of your body? Were you rolling around in it?"

"Look, you hick doctor—it's none of your business how it got there," snarled Muff. "Just give me some medicine and let me get out of here."

Nobody had ever talked to Dr. Pooten that way. Everybody in Pea Ridge loved Dr. Pooten. When people couldn't pay their bill, they would pay with work, fresh eggs, vegetables, or whatever they had.

Dr. Pooten gave Muff a shot in the hip and some calamine lotion, but he also told her to rub alcohol on the affected area every day after her bath.

Hair-raising screams could be heard echoing down the hall of Monahan Dorm every day for a week. It couldn't have happened to a more deserving person.

Chapter 27

Kidnapping Gone Awry

Aunt Fern was, by far, my favorite relative. In her youth, she had been a beauty queen. She married a very rich man, and they had no children. He died at an early age and left her loaded. I would have liked her, even if she weren't rich.

Aunt Fern lived in Nashville, in an old mansion. Occasionally she would get lonely and call me.

"Sadie Rose Marie, ask Mary Grace and Christina, and all of you come on down and spend the weekend with me."

We would cancel whatever we had going on. When we went to Aunt Fern's house, we knew we were going to have fun.

Aunt Fern had glamorous clothes. We would get in her closet and pick whatever we wanted to wear. Then we would all pile in her big old black Cadillac with the high fins and go to the best places in Nashville for dinner, where she would order lobster for all of us.

We were accustomed to eating beans, 'taters, and corn bread, so this was a delicious treat for all of us.

After dinner she would take us to a play or to the opera. The only opera we had ever been to was the Grand Ole Opry.

We couldn't help ourselves—we just had to giggle. The high-falutin' people would give us mean looks because we had zero sophistication. But we learned quickly how to act.

The next day, Aunt Fern would take us shopping and buy all of us new outfits. Then, we would go back to our dorm, happy, well fed, and well clad.

This went on for two years, but the last time we visited, Aunt Fern acted a little strange. She was talking about the government and social security coming to her house for dinner. We thought, "Maybe they did come to dinner," because we knew that she was rich and important.

Aunt Fern also told us that the president's wife had borrowed all of her clothes. We thought that maybe she was talking about the president of the garden club.

By dinner time, though, she was her old self again. We climbed in the Cadillac (Aunt Fern asked Christina to drive), and we went to dinner and the ballet.

After that weekend, we didn't hear from Aunt Fern for a month. We didn't think too much about this, though. We thought she was in Europe, because she would travel any time the urge would hit her.

One day, she called me, and she was crying. "Get me out of this hell-hole!"

I asked her what she was talking about. She said that she was in the Lovely Valley Nursing Home.

"What on earth are you talking about?" I asked. "I thought you were in Europe."

"Your stupid cousin tricked me into signing a paper that makes her my 'power of attorney'. I thought I was just signing the warranty on my new John Deere tractor."

"But Aunt Fern," I said, "you don't really need a John Deere tractor. You have a wonderful gardener. But if you want one, it's fine with me. You've got plenty of money."

"Don't worry; I don't have the tractor anymore. Deenie made me take it back."

Deenie was my cousin, but I hated her guts. I would never admit to being kin to her—not even to Mary Grace and Catherine. First of all, she was butt-ugly. Second, she had the personality of Attila the Hun. She was as mean as a snake, unbelievably sneaky, stinky, and nasty.

How had absolutely horrible, stupid Deenie, put Aunt Fern in a nursing home? We had to do something about that.

I told Mary Grace and Christina the whole story. We made our plans. We would kidnap Aunt Fern out of the nursing home!

Mary Grace would cause a scene. Christina, and I would slip Aunt Fern out of the back door of the Lovely Valley Nursing Home. That was as far as our plans went—and often, plans go awry.

We drove to Nashville and over to Lovely Valley. We went in, and Christina and I found Aunt Fern. She looked different. Her hair was red, not blonde.

"We're getting you out of here," I whispered.

"Thank the Lord," said Aunt Fern.

Mary Grace was in the front office, throwing a fit and complaining to the administrator that the home smelled like pee.

While Mary Grace was complaining, somebody hit Christine in the face with their false teeth. A little trickle of blood ran down her face.

"Let's get her out the back door, quick," I said.

I grabbed Aunt Fern's hand, and we ran. We got in the car and Christina drove around to the front of Lovely Valley to pick up Mary Grace.

Mary Grace jumped in the car, and we burned rubber out of there. Aunt Fern said that she wanted to go home and get her car, and some money.

It was Friday afternoon. We had signed out of the dorm for the weekend, and we had said that we were going home.

As soon as we got to Aunt Fern's house, we knew that she had been robbed. All of her china was gone from her china cabinet. We looked around and saw that all of her silver was gone, as well, and a lot of Aunt Fern's clothes were missing. Aunt Fern had some really fine possessions, and it appeared that most of them were gone.

"Call the sheriff," Mary Grace said.

"Don't do that," said Christina. "They may know by now that we've kidnapped Aunt Fern from Lovely Valley. We could get in some serious trouble."

This made sense. Of the three of us, Christina was best at looking at all sides of a problem and deciding what was the right thing to do.

Aunt Fern was very rich, and money means power. She called her friend Mr. Joe Harrigan and asked him to report that her things had been stolen. She told him the whole story, and she told him that she knew exactly who had stolen her property. She said that Deenie had taken everything, and that she wanted Deenie arrested.

We found out later that Aunt Fern was right, and Deenie got what was coming to her.

"Let me grab a few things," said Aunt Fern. We'd better get out of here. We'll take my car.

The four of us piled in that big Cadillac, with Aunt Fern behind the wheel. It never occurred to me or Mary Grace to ask where we were going.

"Where are we going?" asked Christina.

"I want to go to Chattanooga to see a lawyer friend of mine. He handled all my affairs when Sterling died. He makes sure that criminals are punished to the letter of the law. I hope he can get me out of this mess."

"But Aunt Fern, our mamas are expecting us home tonight," said Christina.

"Well, I'll call them when we get to Ray's office. They won't mind if you're with me," said Aunt Fern. "Wait, I see a filling station up ahead. They probably have a pay phone we can use."

We wheeled in and Aunt Fern called each of our mamas. She assured them that we were in good hands. Each of them said that it was fine for us to be with her, and for us to be back in the dorm by Monday morning. They didn't know that we had kidnapped Aunt Fern.

Up until this point, Aunt Fern was just fine, her old self, except that she was just as mad as a hornet.

Christina's face was still bleeding.

"Why are you bleeding?" asked Aunt Fern.

"Somebody hit me in the head with their false teeth."

"That was Calvin," replied Aunt Fern. "He hits everybody. When I get my mess straightened out, I'm going to get him out of Lovely Valley. I'll give him a job helping around the house.

"Oops, I forgot to take my medicine." Aunt Fern dug around in her purse and found two bottles of pills.

She pulled into the parking lot of a grocery store. She went in and bought Coca-Colas and peanuts for all of us. Then, she used her Coca-Cola to swallow down two yellow pills and one green one.

We headed out to Chattanooga again, and everything was normal.

About an hour down the road, all hell broke loose. Aunt Fern started acting as crazy as a loon. She speeded up to about 100 miles per hour, and she started talking as fast as she could.

"You know, Rock Hudson is coming to see me next week."

"The F. B. I. has hired me to do an investigation on Deenie."

"The Russians have been in my house. They took all of my canned goods and lined them up in the hall."

At this point, we knew we were in serious trouble … but it got much worse.

"Aunt Fern, aren't you tired?" I asked. "Don't you want Christina to drive?"

"No, I don't want that little bleeding beatnik to drive!" shouted Aunt Fern.

Christina started to cry. Christina was so sweet that nobody ever talked mean to her.

About this time, we all figured out that the pills had something to do with Aunt Fern's behavior.

"Let me see your pills," I said.

I was surprised that she willingly started digging around in her purse, but she couldn't find them. We were going about 100 miles per hour, and Aunt Fern was all over the road.

"Sadie Rose, just look in my purse until you find them," she said, as she took her eyes off the road to hand the purse over to me.

"Watch out!" yelled Christina.

Aunt Fern ran off on the shoulder of the road, but she managed to pull the wheels up on the road again. As she jerked the tires back on the road, we started into a skid, and we spun around in the road three times.

"All three of ya'll just shut up!" she shouted.

We weren't talking. We were too scared.

"You're making me nervous," she added.

I dug around in Aunt Fern's purse until I found the two bottles of pills. I recognized both kinds of medicine. One of the bottles said "amphetamines", and they were for weight loss.

I knew they were for weight loss because I had taken them for about a week. I had gone to a doctor in Nashville to see him about a cold, and he told me that I was too fat. This really hurt my feelings, because I just had a cold—I didn't want to change my lifestyle.

I knew what amphetamines would do to a person. I literally did not sleep for an entire week. I was so wired that I couldn't stop talking, and the very sight of food made me want to throw up my toenails. Never in my life have I felt any better than when I was taking those pills.

Aunt Fern had taken two of those pills at the same time. The other kind of pill was Valium for nervousness, and she had taken one of those.

I'm certainly not a doctor, but I just don't think that those two kinds of pills go together.

The other thing I found in Aunt Fern's purse was a gun. I slipped the gun and the medicine out of her purse and gave them to Mary Grace. Then, I handed the purse over the seat to Christina.

I knew I had to think fast, or we'd all probably die.

"Aunt Fern, we're hungry," I said.

"Sadie Rose Marie, you're way too fat. Let me give you some of my pills and then you won't be so hungry," she said. That hurt my feelings, but I didn't argue.

"Mary Grace and Christina are hungry, and they're not fat," I said.

"The bleeding beatnik is a little on the fat side," replied Aunt Fern.

If you're a little on the plump side, you know it, and you don't need somebody to tell you about it. Under different circumstances, I would have given Aunt Fern a piece of my mind, but we were all scared to death.

"There's the Holiday Inn," said Aunt Fern. "Let's get a room and spend the night. There's a supper club next door, and I feel like dancing."

We all agreed to that—anything to get out of that car!

We checked in to the motel. Aunt Fern was the only one with a suitcase. All that Mary Grace, Christina, and I had were the clothes on our back, and they weren't cute—certainly not nice enough for the Holiday Inn. People in those days dressed in their Sunday best if they were going to a motel or hotel.

Christina and I had only stayed in a motel once or twice in our lives, and Mary Grace had to tell us how to act.

"Quit gawking at everything, Sadie. Hold your head up, Christina. Nobody is going to hurt you."

"I've heard bad girls come to motels," said Christina.

"They do," said Mary Grace, "but so do rich people."

I kept admiring the surroundings. "Isn't that flower arrangement pretty. Look how big that chandelier is," I rattled on.

"Shut up!" shouted Aunt Fern. "Quit acting like hillbillies. I've taken you to lots of fine places. Don't you girls have any raising at all? You're really getting on my nerves. I've got a good mind to get out my gun and shoot you."

We knew that Mary Grace had the gun, but we didn't know what Aunt Fern might do, so we just stayed silent.

After we checked in, we went to our room. Mary Grace worked up her nerve and said, "Aunt Fern, we're going to need to borrow some clothes. We can't go to the supper club looking like this."

Aunt Fern's personality had changed again. "Sure, girls," she said, sweetly, "just help yourselves."

I said, "Mary Grace, come in the bathroom with me. I need your advice about some makeup."

We closed the door, and I whispered, "What are we going to do?"

"Let's tie her up and put her in the car and take her back home."

"How are we going to get her out of here?"

"We could wrap her in a sheet."

"Or, we could just call the police."

"That won't work," Mary Grace replied. "Remember, we're wanted for kidnapping. How long will the effects of those pills last?"

"Well, according to my experience—and I just took one a day—I was awake for twenty-four hours straight. She took two of those pills and a nerve pill, so she might be up for two days and two nights, I guess."

"Get out of my suitcase, you bleeding beatnik," shouted Aunt Fern, at the top of her lungs. For some reason, Aunt Fern was meaner to Christina than she was to Mary Grace or me.

Christina started to cry. "But, you said we could borrow some of your clothes."

"Stop your whining. And for God's sake, quit bleeding!"

Christina's face would not stop bleeding. She had to dab it with a Kleenex. We didn't have a Band-Aid.

"Well, let's go to the supper club," said Aunt Fern. I want to dance."

"You want us to go looking like this?" asked Mary Grace.

"Lord, no! Get in that suitcase and get you something to wear. How many times do I have to tell you?"

Like I said before, Aunt Fern had beautiful clothes. They were just not in that suitcase.

We got dressed the best we could, using Aunt Fern's odd selection of clothes. Mary Grace and I wore pretty bed jackets with our pants. We let Christina have the blouse. We all looked passable, but strange.

Aunt Fern changed her dress, and we noticed that she had lost a lot of weight.

"Aunt Fern, how long have you been taking those pills?" I asked.

"Oh, for about two months. Sandra Jones told me about Dr. Neff. I was getting a little fat around the middle, and all my friends are taking them."

"Aunt Fern, Dr. Pooten said that amphetamines are really, really dangerous and for us to not take them," I said.

"Well, he doesn't know what he's talking about. I've never felt better in my life."

I thought to myself that I had better not say any more. I didn't want to piss her off again.

Aunt Fern took a beautiful scarf out of the suitcase and started wrapping it around Christina's bleeding head. Only movie stars wore turbans back then. Christina didn't say anything—she just wore the turban.

Chapter 28

And Things Get Worse

We walked over to the supper club. As soon as we were seated, Mary Grace, Christina, and I went to the ladies' room.

"What are we going to do?" cried Christina.

"I don't know. I was hoping you had an idea," I said.

"When we leave here, we could say that we need a bandage for Christina, and then we could keep driving to Pea Ridge," said Mary Grace.

It wasn't a perfect plan, but it was the best we could come up with.

Aunt Fern stormed into the ladies' room. "What's keeping ya'll so long? Didn't I tell you I want to dance?"

"But we're hungry," I said.

"I've already ordered for us. Go on out there and start eating. I'll be out in a minute."

When we got to our table, the only thing on it was three short glasses of water—only, it wasn't water! We took a swig. I swallowed mine. Christina spit her's back in the glass, and Mary Grace spit her's all over Christina.

"That's not water," Christina sputtered. Alcohol had never touched our lips before this. Years later, I figured out that what we had was straight vodka.

"Quick, we have to do something with the rest of this stuff before Aunt Fern comes back," said Mary Grace.

"Let's pour it under the table," I said. We did, but I accidentally poured mine on Christina's shoes.

By this time, Aunt Fern had come back to the table.

"We need something to eat," I begged.

"Is that all you want to do? Eat? It's no wonder you're so fat!"

I'd had enough. "Aunt Fern, you're hurting my feelings! I'm not fat! A little plump, maybe …"

"My precious little Songbird, I'm so sorry," said nice Aunt Fern. "Let's go dance."

As we walked through the supper club's restaurant section, Mary Grace stole a roll off of someone's plate, and we each had a bite. That was our supper.

I thought I would die of embarrassment when we got out on the dance floor.

Aunt Fern grabbed Christina, pulled her over, and started some sort of wild dance. Mary Grace and I lagged behind.

"Get her purse and give me the car keys," I said. "I'll go get the car and get it as close to the door as possible. I'll leave it running and come back in. I'll help you and Christina get her in the car, and we'll take her home."

When I came back with the car, Mary Grace was still holding Aunt Fern's purse. We grabbed a table cloth and stuffed it down in the purse.

The band started playing *"Hernando's Hideaway,"* a lively tango.

Aunt Fern was holding Christina's hand, and they were doing a perfect tango. Christina looked like she wanted to die.

We signaled Christina to tango Aunt Fern out of the side door. That worked really well, because Aunt Fern had her eyes closed, like she was really "getting into" dancing the tango.

Christina danced her straight out into the parking lot. We threw the table cloth over head. Then, all hell broke loose.

Chapter 29

And Things Get Worse Than You Can Imagine

Aunt Fern realized what we were doing. She started screaming at the top of her lungs and she was flinging her arms all around, trying to get the table cloth off of her head.

A police car drove up with lights flashing. A young police officer got out of the car.

"What do you girls think you're doing?"

"What do you think they think they're doing?" Aunt Fern yelled. "They're trying to kill me! They're killing me! They're killing me!"

The officer pulled his gun out of its holster. He made us put our hands over our heads. When he did this, Aunt Fern jerked the table cloth off of her head.

Her hair looked really funny. Her head looked like it was about to fall off of her shoulders.

The officer patted us down and then he handcuffed us.

"Young ladies, I'm going to have to lock you up," he said.

"Please, no!" begged Christina. "Aunt Fern is crazy. We're just trying to get her home."

"Take those handcuffs off of my sweet Songbirds and the bleeding beatnik," Aunt Fern shouted, as she pulled her wig off of her head and started beating the officer across his face with it.

An older officer pulled up. "Do you need any help?"

"Yes, sir, I believe I do," the young officer said. "I've got a situation here that I can't figure out. These three young ladies in the strange looking clothes had a table cloth over this distinguished looking woman's head, and they were trying to force her into this Cadillac. She said that they were trying to kill her."

Bald-headed Aunt Fern grabbed Mary Grace's purse, dug down in it, and pulled out the gun.

"Young man, I've told you once to get those handcuffs off of my girls!"

"Woman, put that gun down!" the older officer exclaimed. "Are you crazy?"

"Yes, she is!" said Mary Grace. "That's what we've been trying to tell you!"

"Actually, officer, she's not really crazy—she just took two diet pills and a Valium at the same time," Christina said.

"Oh, let me guess. Dr. Neff," said the older officer.

"Yes," said Christina.

"I've dealt with his patients before. He's a quack. He ought to be locked up. My wife drove all the way to Nashville to get some of those pills. She took them for three days, and she wouldn't quit talking. I finally had to flush them down the toilet."

"Sir, this gun isn't real—it's a pop gun," said the young officer.

"Aunt Fern, what are you doing with a pop gun?" I asked.

"I bought it for Sippard, but he hit me in the head with the tire swing, so I decided to keep it for myself," said Aunt Fern.

"Now, let's figure out how to get your aunt back home," said the older officer.

"We'd better get her to Dr. Pooten, down in Pea Ridge," said Christina, as she pushed the turban up to reveal her bleeding head.

"What's wrong with your head?" asked the young officer.

"I bumped it," said Christina.

I had had enough lying. "She did not! We kidnapped Aunt Fern from the Lovely Valley Nursing Home. While we were in there, an old man threw his false teeth at Christina and hit her in the head."

"Kidnapping is a serious offense," said the older officer.

"I know," I said. "I just want this to be over. We're all starving, and we're worn out, and Christina has never told a lie in her life." I was sobbing, now.

"Let me make a phone call," said the older officer.

He went over to his car, and in a few minutes he came back.

"They don't even know that she's gone," he said, "so you girls are off the hook."

We managed to get Aunt Fern into the back seat of the young officer's police car. I rode in the back with her. Christina drove the Cadillac, with Mary Grace riding shotgun, and we headed for Pea Ridge.

Aunt Fern started singing, "You ain't nothing but a hound dog, crying all the time, you ain't never caught a rabbit, and you ain't no friend of mine."

The polite young officer couldn't take it anymore. He turned on the siren and floor boarded it!

Mary Grace and I loved driving fast down a road, but we knew that poor Christina was scared to death. Christina had never driven faster than fifty-five miles per hour in her life.

About halfway between Chattanooga and Pea Ridge, Aunt Fern stopped singing, and she slumped over onto my shoulder. I shook her vigorously, but to no avail. Aunt Fern would not wake up.

"Stop! Stop the car!" I cried. "I think Aunt Fern is dead!"

The young officer pulled the car over to the shoulder of the road. He got out of the car and opened the back door. He tried to wake Aunt Fern up. She was still breathing, but she was out like a light.

He got back in the car and started back to Pea Ridge, as fast as ever. When we got to Pea Ridge, Dr. Pooten met us at the emergency room door. A couple of attendants got Aunt Fern onto a stretcher, and they wheeled her away. We told Dr. Pooten the whole story.

"She'll be fine," Dr. Pooten assured us. "Christina, I think I need to put a couple of stitches in your head."

Three days later, Aunt Fern awakened from her stupor.

"Where am I? How did I get here?"

"You're very fortunate to be here and to be alive," said Dr. Pooten. "You could have killed yourself. Worse still, while you were drugged up, you could have killed the girls."

"What are you talking about? Where am I?"

"You're in the Pea Ridge hospital. You've been here for the last three days."

"Where was I before that?"

"You were in the Lovely Valley Nursing Home."

"What are you talking about? Have you lost your mind?"

"Fern, you're a very smart woman. I can't believe that you were stupid enough to mix Black Beauties and Valium."

"What are Black Beauties?"

"Those are the diet pills you were taking."

"Well, John, I was getting a little fat around the middle. I thought those pills were going to be an easy way to reduce—at least, that's what Dr. Neff said."

"Fern, you're a beautiful woman. However, women who're your age are supposed to be a little thick in the middle. If you want to be a little slimmer, start exercising and cut out the pie."

Aunt Fern stayed in the hospital for a couple of weeks—long enough to become drug free. When she finally got home, she went to Harvey's and bought a very good Playtex girdle.

Next, she had to deal with Deenie. Aunt Fern had her arrested, and Deenie was charged with fraud and theft.

Chapter 30

▼

Rich Girl, Poor Girl

Sparrow Grant was homecoming queen, a cheerleader, rich, and beautiful. Her only problem was—she was as "dumb as a gourd". Sparrow got into trouble with her grades, and she was about to flunk out of college. Her daddy came up to the college and spoke with the Dean of Women. He told the dean that he would withdraw his large contribution to the college if Sparrow had to come home without a degree.

The dean suggested that he hire a tutor for Sparrow.

Mr. Grant asked the dean to tell him who was the smartest student in the college. The dean didn't even have to look in her records—she just said, "George Washington Tucker Green".

Mr. Grant hunted George down, told him he would give him a huge tutorial fee for helping Sparrow, and would give him another huge fee when she passed everything.

George was delighted. In the end, George earned every penny!

Sparrow was not only spoiled, she was very stuck on herself. She drove a brand new Corvette, only dated football players, and only wore designer clothes. Sparrow also did a lot of drinking.

George didn't like her, but he did like being seen with her and all of the attention she got.

I almost gave up hope of marrying George. I simply couldn't compete with the college beauty queen.

George almost worked himself to death trying to make Sparrow maintain a C minus average. Sparrow didn't try to help herself, either. She just expected George to do all the work to get her the grades while she kept on with her partying lifestyle.

Her "football-player-of-the-month" got injured in a game, and he had to be hospitalized. This left Sparrow dateless, at the last minute, for the Country Club dance. She told George that he was taking her to the dance, and George didn't object.

She told George to go back to his dorm room and get ready for the dance, and she would pick him up in thirty minutes in her Corvette.

George got dressed in his best (and only) suit, but at the last minute, he borrowed Jackson's tuxedo coat. The sleeves on the coat were way too short.

Sparrow didn't even look at George when she picked him up. She floor-boarded the 'Vette, and when she pulled into the Country Club driveway, she jumped out of the car, leaving George tagging along behind.

He went in the dance area, looked around, and found Sparrow talking to her daddy. As he walked up, they both ignored him.

When Sparrow finally looked at George and saw what he was wearing, she almost had a stroke.

"What have you got on," she hissed. "Are you trying to embarrass me to death? For God's sake, take off that tuxedo coat! Can't you see that everybody else has on a suit coat? Come over here and sit down!"

George did as he was told. His feelings were hurt, and things only went downhill from there.

When the waiter came by, Sparrow ordered drinks. George knew that he wasn't going to drink any alcohol that night, because he didn't want to make a scene.

Sparrow drank half of her drink and went off to dance with a country club boy. George poured his drink into Sparrow's glass. Sparrow came over to where George was sitting, drank her whole drink, and didn't even sit down.

The waiter came back and asked George what he was going to have for dinner. George didn't recognize anything on the menu, so he ordered the first thing on it, "la-sag-new".

Sparrow dance by, just as George said "la-sag-new"

"Did you hear what he just said," she mocked. "La-sag-new." Then, she doubled over with laughter. Everybody within earshot started laughing, too.

The waiter came over with George's order.

"Here's your 'la-sag-new'. Enjoy."

When George finished his meal, he looked around for Sparrow. He spotted her just as she walked out of the door with the country club boy.

The waiter came over to George and presented him with the enormous bill of $5.95. George didn't have $5.95, nor did he have a ride back to the dorm.

This is the point where my luck turned around.

George went back to the country club kitchen and asked to use the telephone. He called me to come over to the country club to pick him up, and I did.

"Sadie Rose, I have never, in my life, been so humiliated," said George. "Before I tell you everything, I need to borrow $5.95."

"I only have $5.00," I said. "Here, take it."

George dug around in his pants pocket and came up with 74¢. He reached into Jackson's tuxedo coat and found 26¢. He could pay his country club bill—if he didn't have to pay any tax—and still have a nickel left over.

"Sweet Sadie, you don't know how much I appreciate this," said George. "I'll pay you back."

"You bet you will," I thought to myself. "I'm going to marry you."

It would take years and years, but my dream finally came true.

Chapter 31

Good Dorm Life

Some people didn't like Mary Grace and me that much because we caused too much trouble. Everybody loved Christina, though, because she was good.

One of the people who didn't like Mary Grace and me was Miss Raddle, our house mother. She tried very hard to catch us doing something wrong so she could give us demerits and then campus us. We would catch her mumbling to herself, "It's those Songbird girls … they did it!" We came *so* close to getting caught, so many times.

We didn't do really bad things, but we just didn't like to follow rules. We broke the "no cooking in the room" rule all of the time. After all, we had to stretch our budget. When it was close to the end of the week, we had spent most of our money.

We would buy Campbell's soup and crackers, and then we would heat the soup in the popcorn popper. Later on, we had an electric skillet, and boy, we could cook anything in that sucker!

Frozen pizza had just come on the market, and we would cook it in the skillet. The only problem was, it was very aromatic.

When we would cook it, Miss Raddle would smell it. She thought she had caught us red handed.

She knocked on the door just as we were going to do our laundry on the floor below. When she knocked, we piled every one of those clothes on top of the skillet.

"Are you girls cooking?" she asked.

"No, Ma'm," we lied.

She looked around and saw nothing. She finally left, disappointed again. Our clothes were at the point of catching fire. Steam was billowing up. If she had just stayed a little longer, she would have caught us, and we would *really* have been in trouble! Even though we washed our clothes thoroughly, we smelled like pizza for a long time after that.

College was one of my favorite times of life. It was so much fun. My mama supported me, so I didn't have to work. I grew out of my "baby fat", and I was no longer plump. I had Mary Grace and Christina as my special best friends, and I wasn't shy, once I got the hang of having a good time—and I haven't stopped having a good time, yet!

I learned how to study just enough to pass all of my courses and still have a good time. Mary Grace was very smart, and she didn't have to study hard. Good grades came naturally to her. Christina had to work harder than Mary Grace or me, but she made the Dean's List every semester.

Life was good!

Chapter 32

Mad Cat

General was the old tabby tom cat that lived outside our dorm. Miss Raddle hated General. She ran him off every day, and General returned every day.

Miss Raddle warned us that if she ever caught any of us feeding General, she would give us demerits.

We paid no attention to Miss Raddle. General would eat anything, but vodka and chocolate were his favorite food and drink.

Sparrow and Glory turned that old tom cat into a bad alcoholic.

One afternoon, Julia walked past old General, who was passed out under some azaleas. Julia felt sorry for him, so she tucked him under her shirt and secreted him up to her dorm room. Julia's dorm room was two doors down the hall from our room.

When Julia walked in her room, all of us were there, practicing our dance steps. We were slow dancing to Floyd Cramer's *Last Date*.

Julia came in the room and pulled old General from underneath her shirt. He looked really bad, but he was conscious, and he was in a *very* bad mood.

Alice Ivy dug down into her purse and found a nickel. She went down the hall to the candy machine and bought General a Hershey bar.

Glory went down to her room, and she came back with a flask. She took a big swig and then poured the rest of the flask contents in a saucer for General.

Esther came in the room and took one look at old General, and declared that he needed a make-over. Esther loved to give make-overs.

Old General was "sore-eyed", and his coat was matted. Esther started the make-over by giving General a haircut. He was quite drunk, so he didn't object. After the haircut, he looked much better.

Next, Esther drew a bubble bath and put General in it. When the water touched him, General woke up out of his stupor, and he was fighting mad. Julia was standing by with a dry towel.

By this time, General was squirming so much that Esther could hardly hold him. Esther handed General to Julia, and he promptly bit the fire out of her. It was a pretty deep puncture wound, and Julia was bleeding profusely.

Christina started screaming, "We've got to get Julia to the doctor! She could get rabies! You know General hasn't had any shots!"

We wrapped a towel around Julia's hand and got her in the car. Alice Ivy was driving, and we sped over to the hospital emergency room. We put General in a pillow case and took him with us so the doctor could do a rabies test on him.

General was not happy about being in the pillow case! He was hissing and clawing and meowing all the way to the hospital.

We took Julia in the emergency room. When she told the doctor what had happened, he said that we had to find the cat; otherwise, he would have to give her a series of rabies shots. Julia told the doctor that we had the cat and that we had left him in the car.

Mary Grace and I went to the car to get General. When we opened the car door it was too quiet. We should have heard some meowing and hissing out of General.

We opened the pillow case and General was lying there, not moving. He was as dead as a doornail.

We took General in to the doctor. He said, "This is not good. I'll have to box him up and send him to a lab in Nashville to be tested. We don't test dead animals here.

"Julia, you may have to take the shots in your stomach if the cat does have rabies."

The doctor stitched up the puncture wounds in Julia's hand and told her that if she ran a fever or felt bad in any way, to get back to the emergency room immediately. The doctor told her that the results of the lab work would be back to him the next day.

We went back to the dorm. Julia was feeling fine, and she decided to have some fun. She went in her room, got out the toothpaste, and brushed her teeth—but she didn't spit. She put more toothpaste in her mouth and worked up a foamy lather. Then, she staggered into the hall.

Julia's roommate, Viola, started knocking on doors and screaming, "Julia's gone mad! She's got rabies! She's got rabies!"

Julia started biting at some girls who were in the hall, and the girls started running.

Alice Ivy took charge of the situation. She tackled Julia, and they were rolling around on the floor when Miss Raddle came up the steps to see what all the ruckus was about.

"Julia's got rabies," said Christina.

"She's gone mad," said Maggie.

"I warned you about that old tom cat," said Miss Raddle. "Songbirds, I know you're involved in this mess. You're probably the cause of it. I've got you now!"

Miss Raddle hated Mary Grace and me.

"Get off of me," screamed Julia. "I'm not mad, and I don't have rabies!"

Julia and Alice Ivy got up off of the floor.

"I'm sorry, Miss Raddle," said Julia. "I was just playing a little joke."

"But General bit you, and now he's dead," said Miss Raddle. "We need to get you to the emergency room."

"I've already been—see my stitches?" said Julia.

"Did the Songbird girls bring that cat in this dorm?" asked Miss Raddle.

"No," cried Julia,. "I did."

"Humph!" snorted Miss Raddle, and stomped off down the stairs.

The next day the lab results came back. We were relieved to learn that General had died of old age and alcoholism, and Julia didn't have to have those shots in her stomach.

Chapter 33

Alice Ivy Green

Alice Ivy had such a hard time making a decision about what field of study she wanted to major in. She knew that she did not want to be a teacher, a nurse, or a secretary. She started out majoring in pre-med, but quickly found out that dissecting frogs was no more fun than dissecting pig hearts.

Next, she majored in sociology. That lasted one semester. She had to go to a home whose family was on relief. Before she even got in the house, the drunk daddy blasted away at her with a shotgun. Fortunately for Alice Ivy, he had had so many cans of beer that his vision was blurred, and he missed.

Alice Ivy reacted a lot like her mama would have reacted. She chased the drunk man down.

"You sorry, no good slime ball, I'm here to bring your family some food. Why are you shooting at me?" she shouted. Then, she picked up a stick and started beating the man about the legs and buttocks. She almost got put on probation for that.

The Dean of Women told Alice Ivy that she didn't think it was in the cards for Alice Ivy to be a social worker. Alice Ivy completely agreed with her.

After sociology, Alice Ivy tried pre-law. She was the only girl in the class, but this didn't bother her—she just didn't like pre-law. When she had to defend someone that she knew was a guilty criminal, she just couldn't do it. Miss Anna and Miss Lucy had drilled the concepts of right and wrong into her head very thoroughly. When she tried defending someone she knew was guilty, it gave her a sick headache.

By this time, Miss Anna told Alice Ivy that she had come to the end of her rope with Alice Ivy's indecisiveness. "Alice Ivy," she said, "just major in education like every other woman who isn't going to be a nurse or a secretary. It doesn't mean that you *have* to teach, but you will have a degree to fall back on, and that will come in very handy."

Alice Ivy reluctantly agreed.

Because of all the changes Alice Ivy had made in trying to settle on a major, she ended up having to go to school for an extra year. She was now in the same class with Mary Grace, Christina, and me.

Alice Ivy was very pretty, by now, but boys were afraid to ask her out on dates. There were many weekends when she would sit in the dorm because none of the boys had the courage to ask her to go to a movie. George tried to help her out by getting some of his friends to ask her out for a date, but she tended to intimidate the boys—she thought she could do anything a boy could do, including changing the oil in a car or changing a flat tire. She also had a reputation for beating boys or men up for things like calling her "poison ivy" or shooting at her.

Most of the girls who started in Alice Ivy's class when they were freshmen, just out of high school, had graduated from college and had moved to Atlanta to start their careers. Alice Ivy quickly became best friends with Mary Grace, Christina, and me. We shared similar backgrounds, and we had known each other almost all of our lives.

Chapter 34

Christina Goes Crazy

Christina could not stand not being loved by everybody. We tried to explain to her that not everybody was going to love her.

"You don't like everybody you meet, do you?" asked Alice Ivy.

"Well, no—but I pretend I do," answered Christina.

This conversation came after Christina could not get into the newly formed sorority made up of the "brilliant but nerdy" girls. The other sorority that was being formed was made up of "beautiful and rich" girls.

"Maybe if I become a majorette, I can be popular, and then I can get in," said Christina.

"Christina, are you crazy? You have to play an instrument in the band, and then work up to being a majorette," said Mary Grace.

Nothing we said could stop her. Christina joined the beginner's clarinet class in the music department. Christina had never had any music classes in her life. She didn't even learn to play the Tonette in elementary school, and she wasn't in the rhythm band, either.

Christina was not one for giving up, though. She rented a clarinet and started practicing.

It was absolutely awful. There were more squeaks than there were notes, and we had to listen to Christina tooting that horn day and night.

Her tooting did not get one bit better. She took that clarinet everywhere she went and tooted away.

Finally, we just couldn't take it anymore.

"Christina," I said, "you need to practice your marching."

Christina started a two week marching practice schedule. She tried very hard, but she had absolutely no sense of rhythm. She would march back and forth, back and forth, from one side of the dorm room to the other. Her marching did not improve.

Then, Christina bought a baton, and she twirled and twirled and twirled. She practiced throwing the baton in the air, but she dropped it more than she caught it.

We simply couldn't take it anymore.

"Christina, you'll have to wear that uniform with the short skirt, and that might be a sin," I said. I didn't believe a word of this, and I felt badly about resorting to using a guilt trip on her, but we were desperate.

"You don't need to worry," Christina replied. "I'll just pray more."

"Christina, why do you even want to be in the "rich and beautiful" sorority anyway?" asked Mary Grace.

"Because I want them to like me. They don't like me," she whined.

"Well, tough," said Mary Grace. "They don't know what they're missing. You are a wonderful, kind, and sweet person. But you're driving us crazy with all this majorette stuff," I said.

This made Christina cry. I felt awful.

"I'm sorry, Christina," I said. "Please don't cry. We'll figure something out."

Even though we didn't want to be in "rich and beautiful", we told Christina we would try to get us all in the sorority. We loved Christina.

Chapter 35

Drastic Measures

Professor Edwards, the young single band director, had a crush on Mary Grace. He had asked her to meet him in Nashville several times, although it was frowned on for professors to date college girls.

Professor Edwards was not Mary Grace's type, and she turned him down every time.

"Mary Grace, please go out with Professor Edwards and see if you can get Christina in the band," I begged. "Maybe she can be a majorette for one game, or maybe she can just march or carry a flag."

"I'm not going out with him," said Mary Grace.

That night, when Christina got out of class, she started her tooting and marching and trying to twirl the baton. Mary Grace couldn't take it anymore.

"Alright, alright, I give up! I'll do what I can!" she screamed.

The next time Professor Edwards asked Mary Grace out, she agreed to meet him at the China Hut, a new Chinese restaurant that had only been open about six months. All of us wanted to eat at the China Hut, but we couldn't afford it.

Alice Ivy and I said we would drive Mary Grace to the China Hut and drop her off. We said we would shop at the Woolworth Dime Store, and then pick her up in an hour and a half. We told her to try to slip us out a little taste of the food, too.

Mary Grace was not happy, but she went.

Professor Edwards was delighted. He was very nice to Mary Grace. He told her to order whatever she wanted, but she didn't know what any of the dishes were on the menu. She finally ordered Moo Goo Gai Pan, because it just *sounded* Chinese, but she didn't like it very much.

Halfway through dinner, Mary Grace told Professor Edwards about Christina's ambition to be a majorette and how she was driving us crazy with her clarinet tooting and marching and baton twirling. Professor Edwards told her that if she would go out with him again, he would see what he could arrange.

Mary Grace didn't want to have a second date with Professor Edwards, but she agreed, anyway.

Professor Edwards loved being seen with such a radiantly beautiful and smart girl.

The next weekend we followed the same routine: we dropped Mary Grace off at the China Hut and picked her up after an hour and a half.

Mary Grace got in the car.

"I hope you're happy now! The job is done!" she screamed, and threw two fortune cookies at us.

"Was this dessert?" I asked.

"This little cookie sure isn't very good," Alice Ivy said.

"Don't eat the paper on the inside. It tells your fortune," said Mary Grace.

"I'd rather have had chocolate pie," I said.

True to his word, Professor Edwards had told Mary Grace that he had arranged for Christina to march and carry a flag with the band at the next football game.

The next Saturday, Christina put on her borrowed majorette outfit and proudly marched with the band.

This seemed to satisfy Christina.

Now, we would pursue our quest to get in the "rich and beautiful" sorority.

Chapter 36

Nurse Wood

Mama insisted that I make a career choice. I had already told her I wanted to be a teacher, but she said I should try out other things before I made a life-long decision.

I had three choices: teacher, nurse, or secretary. Or, I could have been a housewife, but I wasn't ready to stay home all day with a house full of babies and clothes to wash.

Being a teacher was my first choice, and being a nurse was my second,—but I fainted at the sight of blood. I knew I didn't want to be a nurse, but Mama insisted that I give it a try.

The only advantage of getting a part-time job at the hospital was seeing George Washington Green, who came by often. I loved George, ever since he took Mary Grace, Christina, and me to the prom.

By this time I had figured out that I didn't want a "pretty boy".

Being a secretary was my third choice, but I couldn't type worth a dime, and I didn't think I wanted to carry coffee to the boss.

So, I went by the hospital, hoping there wasn't a part-time job available.

As luck would have it, Dr. Pooten hired me on the spot. I would work one hour a week—not much, but surely it would make Mama happy.

I would work on Mondays, from 3:00 to 4:00. That would work out fine, because I didn't have class then.

I would get out of class, drive to Pea Ridge, work my one hour, and go back to the dorm. Surely I would run into George every once in a while.

I didn't ask any questions. I just told Dr. Pooten that I would see him on Monday.

I thought that maybe I'd get to wear one of those beautiful starched white uniforms and a cute little nurse's hat. I hoped I would get to deliver snacks to the patients. I could smile and push a cart. That could be fun.

Wow, was I wrong!

When I reported on Monday, Cleo Wood, a mean spirited nurse, gave me an awful gray sack uniform, and then she told me what I was to do. She was grouchy, and I was afraid of her.

"You'll be emptying patients' bed pans," she said.

"But, I might throw up," I said.

"Too bad," she said. "Now, get busy."

As you can imagine, bed pan duty was just awful. I thought I might see George Washington, but he wasn't there.

I gagged for half an hour, and then I figured out that if you poured disinfectant in the bedpan and covered it with toilet paper, I could pretend I was carrying something besides somebody's body waste.

Nurse Cleo was not at all happy with my decision.

"Who told you to do that?" she yelled at me.

"Nobody. I just thought ..." But she didn't let me finish my sentence.

"Who told you to think?" she asked. "You think you're better than anybody else, just because you're in college," she yelled.

Nurse Wood was the head of all the practical nurses in the hospital. Their duties were: delivering food, bathing the patients, emptying bed pans, and mopping up messes—certainly, nothing glamorous.

Most women were housewives and mothers. Women like Nurse Wood, who were at the bottom of the work force with crappy jobs and low pay, were not exactly happy with prissy-butt college girls.

I collected my pay—$1.00—and I hoped that next Monday would be better. Maybe, just maybe, George would be there.

Chapter 37

Thadamus

The next Monday was worse than I could have ever imagined. I had bathing duty, and it wasn't ladies, either!

Nurse Wood had it in for me.

"Miss Uppity, you can bathe Thadamus Cloud," she said.

Thadamus Cloud had had a tractor accident, and half of his right foot got cut right off.

I said that I didn't see why he couldn't bathe himself. This did not please Nurse Wood or Thadamus Cloud.

About this time, I looked outside in the hallway, and I spotted George.

I thought, "I'll just wash Thadamus' face and arms, and then I'll change back into my cute clothes and try to figure out how to talk to George Washington without it being obvious."

My plan didn't work. I washed Thadamus' face and arms. As I was putting away the wash basin and the wash cloth, Thadamus shouted, "She didn't wash me all over!"

Nurse Wood said, "Miss Uppity, wash him all over!"

Well, I washed his chest without looking at him. When I got to his boxers, I thought to myself, "I can't do this—I just can't do it!"

Just as I put the wash cloth on his belly button, Thadamus shouted "*boo!*" at the top of his lungs.

I screamed and dropped my wash pan. Water splashed all over Thadamus' bed, the floor, and me. I ran out of the room as fast as I could and into Dr. Pooten's office.

"Dr. Pooten," I sobbed, "I quit! I have never even seen a naked man, I have never touched one, and I have certainly never washed one!"

"Calm down, Sadie," Dr. Pooten said in his usual calm voice. "What are you talking about?"

"Nurse Wood tried to make me wash Thadamus Cloud all over. I won't do it! I just won't do it!" I kept sobbing.

"She did what?" Dr. Pooten asked.

"She tried to make me wash Thadamus Cloud while he was *uncovered*!"

"She never should have done that to you," Dr. Pooten apologized. "I'll have a talk with her."

Miss Anna walked in Dr. Pooten's office about that time.

"What's the matter, Sadie?" she asked.

"Nurse Wood tried to make me wash Thadamus Cloud all over," I was still sobbing.

"I thought you wanted to be a teacher," Miss Anna replied. "Why are you working here at the hospital?"

"I only worked an hour last week, and a half hour today, because Mama wanted me to. She said I needed to try something else before I made a life-long decision about a career, and I was only trying to make Mama happy," I said.

"I'll call Lou Zena if you want me to," said Miss Anna.

"I'd appreciate it," I said. "I don't want her to be mad at me."

To my horror, George Washington walked in. My gray sack uniform was wet, my hair was a mess, and I was crying.

"Sadie Rose Marie, what on earth happened," asked George.

"Nothing," I blubbered.

"George, why don't you take Sadie to the Dairy Dip and buy her a sundae? She's had a hard day," said Miss Anna.

"Sure," said George. "I'd love to."

I went to change out of my gray sack dress, and as I passed Thadamus Cloud's room, I looked in. Nurse Wood was mopping up the mess I had made. She had done me wrong, but I still felt sorry for her.

Chapter 38

Boots

Jackson Brown and George Washington were very good friends. We all hung out together in the same crowd. They liked being with the "big hair girls".

Jackson was a very enterprising young man. He knew how to make money without working too hard. He always had more money than the rest of us put together.

Jackson would type term papers for slow typists. If a student didn't have a car, Jackson would run a taxi service. Jackson owned a tuxedo, and if a boy needed a tux to impress his girlfriend, Jackson would rent his out. Jackson was the only boy I ever knew who owned his own tuxedo. He was absolutely brilliant.

One Saturday night, we were all hanging out at the Shoney's Big Boy Drive In.

Jackson said, "I read in the paper that there's an auction on Valley Road. I'd kinda like to go."

That got George excited. "Let's go!" he shouted. "We'll all go with you."

When we got there, we started to listen to the auctioneer. He was *good*! He had his patter down—"Who'll give me five, give me five, five, SOLD to the gentleman on the right!"

The gentleman on the right had just bought a rocking chair. The next item was a set of old-timey flat irons. Jackson bid $2.00 and bought the irons.

"I know I can double my money on these," he said.

The next lot that came up was a box of brand new boots. The auctioneer started the bid at $10.00. Jackson bid the ten, and someone else bid $15.00. Jackson countered with $20.00 and the other man passed him with $21.00. Jackson was the only one of us who had $20.00.

Jackson bid $22.00 and the other man said that the bidding was getting too rich for his blood, so he dropped out.

"Sold!" yelled the auctioneer.

Jackson didn't have $22.00—he only had $20.00.

The auctioneer said, "Give me $20.00 and the two flat irons, and the boots are yours."

"I know I can double my money on the flat irons," Jackson said. But none of us had an extra $2.00, even when we pooled all of our money.

"Take it or leave it," said the auctioneer.

"I'll take it," said Jackson, and he gave the auctioneer $20.00 and the flat irons. "I know I can get $3.00 a pair for these boots—easy."

The excitement of getting 43 pairs of boots for $20.00 and two flat irons was too good of a deal to pass up. Dollar signs were flashing in Jackson's eyes.

The next morning we got together again to look over the boots. We were all planning to buy at least one pair each.

I found the boot I wanted to buy. It was beautiful, black alligator, but it was too big. I was willing to buy it, though, because I could stuff toilet paper in the toe. I looked through the whole box, but I couldn't find its match.

Alice Ivy looked through the box, too, for her match, and she couldn't find the right size.

All of us looked closer, and we soon realized that the boots were all the same size. Then we discovered that there wasn't a matching pair in the whole box. All the boots were for the left foot!

Jackson was so mad that his face was turning almost purple. "What am I going to do with 86 boots, all the same size, and all for the left foot?"

"I'll bet these are store samples," said Alice Ivy.

"Maybe we could sell them as flower pots," said Christina.

George and I had the same thought at the same time. "Thadamus," we said together.

"Thadamus Cloud," said George. "He lost half of his right foot in a tractor accident. He refuses to wear anything but a bedroom shoe on his right foot—he's afraid he'll lose his relief money." (Relief was what we called "welfare").

"I'm never speaking to Thadamus Cloud again, as long as I live," I said.

"What did he do to you?" asked George.

"Nothing," I said.

"We can get Alice Ivy to sell him the boots," said George.

"I'm not doing it," Alice Ivy said. Thadamus Cloud is not right!"

"How about Mama?" asked George.

We all knew Miss Anna's reputation for nosing into everybody's business. She loved a challenge like this.

Alice Ivy, George, and I drove over to Pea Ridge that afternoon. I would find every opportunity I could to be with George.

Miss Anna said that her friend, Rachael, was a social worker. "Rachael goes to Thadamus' house every week," Miss Anna said.

The next week, on Wednesday, Rachael went to Thadamus' house. Thadamus bought every one of those boots for $44.00.

Both Jackson and Thadamus were very happy. Jackson had doubled his money, and Thadamus wore a brand new boot for the next 86 days.

Chapter 39

It Wasn't Gabriel's Trumpet

Mary Grace and I put ourselves in charge of Christina's social life. Christina was the most serious of the three of us.

We had never been on vacation. It was spring break, and we had saved our money. We wanted to go to Florida, but there was no way we could do this—we didn't have enough money.

Mary Grace, Christina, and I told our parents that we were going to Nashville to do some shopping, and then we were going to spend two nights with Christina's sister, Hattie. Hattie was as honest and as good as Christina, but we convinced her to lie for Christina if she needed to. Hattie was to tell Christina's parents (if they called) that Christina had gone out for a few minutes, and that everything was fine. Christina's daddy was old, and he could be a pain in the butt.

We decided we would go to Gatlinburg. We only had enough money to spend two nights, if we stretched it.

We signed out of the dorm—destination: home—got our suitcases, and started toward Gatlinburg.

Christina said, "This isn't the way to Hattie's house."

I was driving my normal speed—90 miles per hour.

"Yes it is," I said. "This is a short cut."

I drove for two hours, making good time. We didn't have a clue about Gatlinburg. We didn't know what was there or what to expect.

I pulled over in the parking lot of a country store, and we put the top down. We went in the store, and we all got a Coca Cola and a package of peanuts. We poured the peanuts in the Coca Cola and got back in the car.

"You drive awhile," I told Christina.

By this time, Christina knew we weren't going to Hattie's house. She had grumbled for the past fifty miles, and I was tired of it. I thought that if she was driving, it would shut her up.

"Ya'll are going to get me in trouble. You always get me in trouble. I try to be good and make my parents proud of me, and you always get me in trouble," she mumbled.

"You always have fun, don't you?" asked Mary Grace.

"Yeah, I guess so," Christina admitted.

"We told Hattie what we're doing, and she said she'd cover for you," I said.

Christina was by far the best driver of the three of us. She drove like an old lady ... both hands on the wheel ... 50 miles per hour.

"Can't you drive any faster than this?" asked Mary Grace. "Our vacation will be over by the time we get there."

"Pass those cars," I said.

"I'm not passing anybody! There's a yellow line in our lane. That means, "don't pass", said Christina.

I sat back and read signs.

"Black Bear Hiking Trail," I read aloud. "Raft The River—$5.00."

"What's all this about?" asked Mary Grace.

"I don't know," I said.

"Where are we going?" asked Christina.

"Gatlinburg," said Mary Grace. "You're slow! Haven't you figured that out yet?"

"I am not, and what's in Gatlinburg, anyway?" Christina replied.

"I don't know," I said. "I've never been there."

We had been driving a crooked, curvy, two-lane road for a long time. We were all hungry, tired, and grouchy.

"Feed The Live Bear," I read aloud. "See The Ten Foot Snake."

Rafting, hiking, feeding bears, snakes—nothing on the signs interested me at all. I absolutely didn't want to buy a hand crafted chenille bed spread or a real Cherokee Indian headdress.

"I'm not sure this is going to be much fun," said Mary Grace.

"Me either," I said.

"Lookie there, girls, it's beautiful," said Christina.

"What," Mary Grace and I said at the same time.

"The mountains are lovely," said Christina. The scenery is breathtaking. Look how high the mountains are."

"We have beautiful scenery in Pea Ridge," I said.

"We can walk in the woods any time we want to," said Mary Grace.

"We can float down Cripple Creek in an inner tube whenever we want to," I said, "and who wants to feed a bear, anyway?"

"Hold on, girls," said Christina, who was tired of our bad attitude, "you are the ones who tricked me. I like it here, so hush!"

"Gatlinburg—eight miles," I read.

"Maybe we'll meet some cute guys," said Mary Grace.

Suddenly we came to a screeching halt. You could see nothing but stopped cars for miles.

"I guess there's a wreck up ahead somewhere," said Christina.

None of us had ever seen traffic like that. We were creeping along when Christina started blowing the horn.

"Christina Faith, stop blowing the horn," I shouted. "You can see that those people in front of us can't go anywhere."

Christina raised both of her hands off of the steering wheel. "I'm not doing it!"

"Pull over," said Mary Grace.

"I can't," shouted Christina. "There's a gully over there that goes down a mile, and there isn't a turnout on the side of the road."

"What are we going to do?" I asked.

"Honk, honk, honk," the horn kept blaring.

People were starting to stare at us. Then they started sticking their heads and fists out of their cars.

"Stop blowing you horn, you stupid hussy," shouted the man in the car in front of us.

I pointed to the people in the car behind us. "It's them!"

Nobody believed me, and the horn kept on honking.

Two really cute guys got out of their car and started walking toward us. They looked mad, until they got a look at Mary Grace. Then, they started smiling.

"Our horn won't stop blowing," said Christina.

"Well, let's have a look under the hood," said cute boy number one.

He opened the hood and looked at the motor. He jiggled a few wires. The horn kept blowing.

We heard a loud crash up ahead. Our blowing horn had made one car load of people so nervous that they ran into the rear end of another car. Both car loads of people got out of their cars. They were mad, and they were cussing at each other. This held up traffic worse than before. For miles, all you could see were cars, both in front of us and behind us.

People were starting to walk toward our car.

"Let's put the top up," I said, as I started unsnapping the top cover.

Apparently the cute boys who couldn't get our horn to stop blowing had messed up the convertible top, too. After we got the top cover unsnapped and we pushed the button to put the top up, the top started to go up and down, up and down, and we thought things couldn't get worse.

An older man in overalls got out of his pickup truck and walked back to our car.

"You 'uns got a problem, don't ye?"

"We sure do," we all said at the same time.

"About a mile up the road there's a turn off to the right. Bubba Webb has a shop up there. He works on cars, and he can probably help ya'll. You 'uns just turn right at the next side road."

"I don't think we can wait that long," I said. "We're getting low on gas."

Mary Grace had an idea. "There's not much traffic leaving Gatlinburg. Maybe we can pass those cars and get up to Bubba's."

"Maybe so," said the farmer.

Chapter 40

Hold Your 'Taters

Mary Grace stopped traffic on the left side of the road. I got everybody on the right side of the road to back up one car length. They were glad to do it because they were tired of our horn blowing.

Christina drove. We turned on the dirt road, and after about a half mile we saw Bubba's garage. We sped up the driveway, our horn still blowing, and our top still going up and down.

Bubba came out. "Hold your 'taters, girls."

All three of us got out of the car. "We're not doing it," I said.

"The horn is stuck, and the top won't quit going up and down," said Christina.

Bubba raised the hood of the car, and within five minutes the horn stopped blowing and the top was up.

"Just a little short in the wires," said Bubba.

"How much do we owe you?" asked Christina.

"I ain't gonna charge you for that," said Bubba.

"I can't tell you how much I appreciate your fixing my car," I said.

"Wadden nothin'" said Bubba.

God bless the country boys of the U. S. A.!!!

Bubba had on overalls and no shirt, a greasy bill cap, brogans, and his fingernails were dirty. He looked mighty fine to me.

Country boys are usually "raised-right". They are polite to girls and old people. They can do all sorts of useful stuff, like change a tire, siphon gas, and lift heavy objects. They aren't afraid to get dirty or of hard work.

Bubba reminded me a lot of Hoss. One time, when I was little, I fell down and showed my step-ins. Hoss picked me up out of the mud. He looked at the laughers straight in the eyes and said, "Shut up, or I'm going to knock your teeth out!"

I didn't even get teased about showing my step-ins.

We told Bubba that we were low on gas. He siphoned some out of his dump truck into our car.

"I can get you back on the road, if you'll give me a few minutes," he said.

Christina said, "We would really appreciate it."

Bubba went inside his house and came back with three pieces of chocolate cake on a piece of wax paper.

"Are ya'll hungry?" he asked.

"Starving," we all said.

That was the best cake I've ever eaten in my life.

"Let's go back to Hattie's", said Christina.

We all agreed to that.

Bubba got us back to where we needed to be by leading the way in his dump truck. Nobody wanted to tangle with a dump truck.

Chapter 41

▼

Sitting Up With the Dead—Part 1

Our family had a few normal people, but when we had any kind of family function like a wedding, or a funeral, or a shower, we always put the crazy people in charge.

Our family had its share of crazy, odd, and downright weird people. One was Deenie, my cousin. I hated her!

When Aunt Dot died, Deenie carried on so that you would have thought she liked her. Deenie hadn't seen Aunt Dot in years, but when she heard about Aunt Dot's death, she cried all day—and then she started giving orders!

First of all, Deenie said that she couldn't sit up with the body because she might "have a spell". It was customary, in our part of the country, for someone in the family to sit up all night with the corpse.

Nobody in the family could stand Deenie, but they would let her be the boss of everything to keep her from flying into a rage.

Deenie said that she was in charge of the food, and that everybody was supposed to take all of the food to her house. Of course, she didn't cook, and she just wanted to keep the leftovers. Funeral food is good, and she planned on feeding her own family before anybody else got to her house.

She told our out-of-town relatives to stay with Mama and me because she didn't want to mess up her house. When she told that to Mama and me, we laughed our heads off. Deenie was the worst housekeeper alive! You could smell her house, even before you got inside. I had never eaten a bite of food at Deenie's, and I never intended to. I had only been in her house once, and believe me—once was enough!

Deenie dictated the food that everybody was supposed to bring to her house. I was told to bring hominy. I had tasted hominy once, and I didn't know a single person who liked it.

Deenie did that on purpose. She didn't want anybody to like my food—just being mean, trying to hurt my feelings. Deenie hated me even more than I hated her!

Aunt Inez, Aunt Dot's sister, stayed at our house before the funeral. She was not a good house guest. She dipped snuff, she was wacky, and she forgot why she was at our house. Her clothes were awful. She was going to wear her wedding dress with a pair of pants under it, and a raggedy hat that was draped with fruit. In the end, she had to wear some of my clothes.

Mama was a very gracious hostess, and she made me behave myself.

We got Aunt Inez all dressed up in my clothes (which I donated to her after the funeral—I didn't want them back!) and we took her to the funeral home. She had no idea where she was.

That's another thing we did in our family. We dressed our crazy people up and took them to functions—parading them around for all to see.

Chapter 42

Sitting Up With the Dead—Part 2

For the life of me, I saw no reason to sit up with the dead in the middle of the twentieth century, but it's what we did in our family. Grandma Rose Lena said that our people had done this since she was a little girl, and before she was born, too.

Here's what she told me, and it made good sense back then. But now, I think it's just a tradition that makes no sense—something like throwing salt over your left shoulder after you've spilled it.

Anyway, Grandma Rose Lena said that in the last century, and in the first part of the twentieth century, there weren't any funeral directors like we have today—just people in the community who didn't mind dealing with corpses, so they made those people undertakers.

When a person died, they weren't embalmed like we do it today. The dead person was just placed in a casket (usually a pine box) and was buried after about three days.

The relatives of the dead person waited a few days before burial because there were times when the dead person wasn't actually dead—just in a kind of a coma. So, a relative would sit up with the dead, just in case the dead person was really in a coma and came out of it before the burial.

Mama said I could choose between sitting up with Aunt Dot or staying home with Aunt Inez. I begged Mama not to have to do either one. I knew better than to say, "No" to Mama, but I really didn't want to do either one. Mama said she would make the decision for me, and it was sit up all night long in the funeral home.

Deenie tried to make us bring Aunt Dot's body to our house and have it in our parlor for the viewing. Mama said, "No", and Deenie threw a fit and had a spell. But Mama stood her ground and the viewing was at the funeral home.

I don't know how I did it, but I persuaded Mary Grace, Christina, and George to sit up with Aunt Dot with me. We planned to stay upstairs with Vernon, whose daddy was the funeral director, for as long as we could. Vernon was a good friend of ours, and we had been to the funeral home many times.

When we visited Vernon, we mostly stayed upstairs in the family's living quarters. A few times he took us on a tour of the funeral home, and once he even took us down in the basement to the embalming room.

When we were little, Vernon scared me so bad that I peed in my britches. Vernon was showing us the casket room where they had all the caskets on display. When we weren't looking, Vernon slipped into a casket. As we walked past the casket, he sat straight up and yelled, "*boo!*"

Vernon's daddy had a wooden leg. His leg was shot off in World War II. When we were little, Vernon's daddy scared us, too, because his wooden leg made a loud, thumping noise when he walked.

Now that we were grown, though, we could be more dignified. Aunt Dot was all laid out in her casket, looking better than she had ever looked in her life.

In small towns, almost everybody comes by the funeral home to pay their respects. The turnout was good for Aunt Dot.

Mrs. Bertie Judkins brought one of her famous burnt sugar funeral cakes to the funeral home for the family and guests to enjoy. When nobody was looking, George slipped the cake upstairs. Deenie asked George where the cake was, and George said that he guessed all the visitors ate it all. Deenie was put out and said she wanted to take the cake home with her—but she didn't throw a fit or have a spell.

After all of the friends and family left, Uncle Alonzo stretched out on a davenport and he was asleep in about five minutes. Mary Grace, Christina, George, and I went upstairs to hang out with Vernon.

We ate that entire cake while we talked about college and played with the cat. Vernon got out his Monopoly game, and we played Monopoly until midnight.

Then, Vernon's daddy clumped into the room and told us that we needed to go back downstairs and sit with Aunt Dot.

It wasn't that we were disrespectful—but sitting in that viewing room with the lights down low was pretty creepy. Uncle Alonzo was snoring so loud, it's a wonder he didn't wake Aunt Dot up!

We walked around the viewing room and looked at all the flowers. We tried not to look at Aunt Dot, so we sat down across from Uncle Alonzo and whispered for awhile.

It was 3:00 A. M. and all four of us were dozing off, when a very strange thing happened. Mary Grace woke us up.

"Aunt Dot said something," she said. "I heard a noise coming from the casket."

George had his arm around me and I had my head lying on his shoulder, making progress on my plan to marry George.

"Mary Grace, are you crazy? Aunt Dot is dead," I said. I wanted to get back to cuddling up with George.

"She's serious," Christina said. "I heard it, too."

We all got very quiet and then we heard the noise. It sounded kind of like a moan. We looked at the casket, and Aunt Dot's chest was moving.

"She's alive! We've got to tell somebody," I shouted.

Miss Anna was always the first choice when any of us had any kind of a problem.

We got in the car and drove to Miss Anna's house as fast as we could. We went running into the house, and Alice Ivy came out of her bedroom, armed with a baseball bat. Miss Anna came out of her bedroom swinging a broom.

"What on earth? You've scared us half to death," said Alice Ivy.

Miss Anna swung her broom at George. "This had better be an emergency!"

"It is," we all said together.

"Aunt Dot is alive," I said.

"We all heard her moan and saw her move," said Christina.

"There's got to be a logical explanation," said Miss Anna.

Miss Anna grabbed her coat and put it on over her gown. Alice Ivy just wore her pajamas. They got in Alice Ivy's car and drove to the funeral home with us in the car right behind them.

We went in the funeral parlor and sure enough, Aunt Dot was still making noises and moving.

We were making quite a ruckus. Vernon's dad came clumping into the viewing room.

"What on earth is going on down here?" he demanded.

"Aunt Dot is making moaning noises, and she's moving," said Christina.

"That's impossible," said Mr. Ranger as he walked over to the casket. Then, he took a step back when he saw Aunt Dot move.

I was so scared that I thought *I* might die!

He put his hand on Aunt Dot's body. We couldn't look.

"Here's the problem," said Mr. Ranger. He pulled Vernon's cat out of the casket.

"I'm so sorry," he said. "Tom must have gotten out. What can I do to make it up to you?"

"Tell everybody to bring the food to Sadie's house instead of Deenie's house," said Alice Ivy.

"Better still," said Miss Anna, "tell them to bring it to John Pooten's house. Tell them to bring whatever they want to bring and stay for lunch. We might as well just have a party. After all, Dot was ninety years old and she had a good life—so let's celebrate it!"

I loved Miss Anna for that.

Chapter 43

Odd Behavior

My Grandma Lizzy was extremely unpleasant and odd. First of all, she was very, very clean. She was Deenie's grandma, also, and Deenie was very, very nasty.

When Grandma Lizzy dusted, which was twice a day, she went through a ritual. When she moved a lamp or a trinket, she had to put it back in exactly the same place.

"Precisely, precisely, one, two, three, precisely, precisely, one, two, three," she would mumble, almost inaudibly. She also had to wash her hands all of the time in clean water. This was quite inconvenient, since she had to draw water from the well.

Grandma Lizzy could not cook. If you were unfortunate enough to get hungry at her house, she would give you a weenie out of the package in the refrigerator and a piece of stale light bread.

Grandma Lizzy's husband was odd, too. He saw visions. He would go into the woods to dig for ginseng, and he wouldn't be seen again for days. He didn't talk about anything except his visions.

I had a favorite uncle who was a little strange, too. He could divine water with a forked stick, and he could cure warts.

I absolutely loved Uncle Wheeler. He was a tiny man, and at night he would sit on the porch and listen to a preacher on the radio. When Uncle Wheeler wasn't working the farm during the day, he would sit on the porch and read tracts that he ordered from the preacher.

When I was little, Uncle Wheeler would always have a "play pretty" for me.

One of Deenie's nasty little children chewed her hair all of the time, but this didn't really compare to one of Deenie's nieces.

Deenie had one sister who was very nice—when she was well. Most of the time, though, she was very nervous. She would sit on the porch swing and wrap a handkerchief around her left index finger. When she ran out of cloth, she would unwrap the finger and wrap it again, hour after hour.

Deenie's sister, Tina, passed her nervousness down to one of her children. The child would pull her hair out, one hair at a time, and she always had at least one bald spot at all times. She would pull a hair out, look at it, and then pull out another one.

I've already told you about Uncle Alonzo, who liked to sit up with the dead. Uncle Alonzo enjoyed peas of all kinds—Crowder peas, English (green) peas, butter peas, and even butter beans. He loved to eat all kinds of peas with a knife.

Today, we have names for those disorders and behaviors that were a little out of the norm. Back then, we just called the folks who had them "curious people".

Chapter 44

▼

Silver Spoons

When we arrived at our college campus as freshmen, there were no fraternities or sororities at the school. Sparrow's alcoholic mother decided that since she had gone to one of the "finest schools on the East coast", and since she had belonged to a "rich girl sorority", then Sparrow had to be in a sorority, too.

Sparrow's mother enlisted her country club friends to help her get the project off the ground. Then, she told Sparrow's daddy that she would expose his "dirty little secret" unless he wrote a huge check to the college to start a sorority.

Sparrow's daddy didn't want his business partners to know that he had been stealing from the company for years, so he wrote the check.

The college president told him that the college couldn't have sororities for the girls without fraternities for the boys. The president also said that the college would need an honorary fraternity and sorority, and a social fraternity and sorority, so that was how our college ended up with four "Greek" organizations—one each for the "rich and beautiful (or handsome)" and one each for the "brilliant but nerdy".

Mary Grace and Alice Ivy could have been in the "smart girl" sorority if they had been willing to study that hard, but they weren't willing. Christina and I didn't have a snowball's chance in hell of getting in that sorority.

Glory got in "rich and beautiful" because her daddy was superintendent of schools where Sparrow had graduated.

Sparrow had gotten kicked out of several private schools and had to graduate from a public school. She got in some serious trouble because of her bad attitude and poor grades.

Glory's daddy did some fancy footwork to make sure Sparrow got her high school diploma, and now it was payback time. Mr. Johnson, Glory's daddy, strongly suggested to Sparrow's daddy that Glory be invited to join the "rich and beautiful" sorority. Glory insisted that "rich and beautiful" also "rush" Alice Ivy, Mary Grace, Christina, and me.

Sparrow's sorority friends were just like her. They decided that they would make the initiation so bad that we would not want to join. Sparrow and her friends made sure we knew our place and that we stayed in it.

Christina was making us tuna fish sandwiches for lunch when Sparrow and her friends walked by our dorm room.

"Look, the hillbillies are eating cat food. That's what we feed our cats," said one of the girls.

Sparrow and her friends were doubled over with laughter.

"It's tuna fish," said Mary Grace. "Haven't you ever eaten tuna fish?"

"We're not hillbillies," they all shouted.

Mary Grace was so mad.

"Maybe they don't know they're hurting our feelings," said Christina.

"Christina," said Mary Grace, "if you think someone is trying to hurt your feelings, they are. It's not an accident."

"I told Sparrow that I like her car," said Christina.

"What did she say?" asked Mary Grace.

"That it's very expensive."

When Muff Mobley didn't want to do her laundry, she would go into our closets and steal our clothes. Muff was trying to get into "rich and beautiful", too. She had on one of Christina's outfits.

All of us had cute clothes. Our mamas made them from the Butterick pattern book, except for Alice Ivy. Alice Ivy had ready-made clothes because Miss Anna couldn't sew.

"What are you wearing?" one of Sparrow's friends asked Muff. "It doesn't look like it came out of the Bobbi Brooks store to me."

"I'll bet you didn't even get it at Harvey's," said Sparrow.

Muff said that the outfit she had on belonged to Christina, and she was wearing it because all of her designer clothes needed washing.

"Looks like it's made out of a flour sack to me," said Sparrow's friend.

For the life of me, I didn't know what had gotten into Christina. Why on earth would she want to be around such snotty and uppity people?

Christina asked Sparrow and her friends what our initiation was going to be. She then added, "You know I'm a majorette, don't you?"

Sparrow and her friends made our initiation so disgusting that we turned them down before they had the chance to turn us down.

For our initiation, the "rich and beautiful" said we had to wear no brassiere for a week. This would have been fine for Mary Grace and Christina, who were well endowed. Alice Ivy and I would have looked like twelve year old boys.

If that wasn't bad enough, they also said that we could not have big hair for a week. We had to be "flat-heads".

Then, they said we had to eat pig brains.

We knew we were not doing any of this.

On top of all that, we had to pay $200.00 as our initiation fee. Our parents didn't have that kind of money to spend on foolishness.

Chapter 45

Alice Ivy Speaks Out

Alice Ivy was not a wimp, and she was not the kind of girl that people can treat badly. It was very plain that she did not like what was being dished out at this sorority initiation. We weren't surprised that she spoke out—we were only surprised that she had held her tongue for as long as she did.

Now it was time for her to speak her mind. She had had enough uppity and snotty behavior from the "rich and beautiful".

At the meeting of the "rich and beautiful" sorority after rush and what would have been our initiation—had we chosen to join the sorority—we all marched ourselves into the sorority meeting room. Alice Ivy got the microphone and made a brilliant speech.

"Girls," she said, "I would like to point out a few things to you. I have known most of you for four years, now. Joining this sorority, which all of you so want to be in, requires a great deal of thought on our part.

"You girls are never going to be the real 'rich and beautiful's' equal, no matter how hard you try. The really 'rich and beautiful' will always think that they are so much better than you. That is why my friends and I have chosen not to join your sorority."

Everybody gasped!

Alice Ivy took a deep breath and continued. "How do you 'rich bitches' get off thinking that you're better than us? Our parents have worked their fingers to the bone, trying to give us a good education.

"Sparrow, you wouldn't even be here if it wasn't for your daddy's money and if George Washington hadn't helped you to maintain your "C minus" grade average.

"You have treated us like underlings. You have made fun of our clothes and our tuna fish, for God's sake. Your kind will never get what you deserve, but I hope I have raised your awareness as to what people really think about you.

"I'll have you know that all of us—the ones you made so much fun of—are from raised-right, honest, clean, hardworking families. This is something we're very proud of!"

Mary Grace, Christina, Glory, and I started to applaud.

The "rich bitches" didn't like this one bit! They tried to interrupt Alice Ivy and object, but she continued.

"My daddy, and other daddies, died fighting for this country and for you to have the freedom to go to school and make something of yourselves without any dictator telling you that you had to go to work in a factory or something. Now you look down on us like we're piss ants. You feel like all you have to do is to just flick us off, and we'll go away. Well, I'm here to tell you, we "piss ants" have got some long stingers, and you don't want to mess with us!"

Glory and five other girls were the first to leave. After Christina, Mary Grace, Alice Ivy, and I left the sorority house, there were only fifteen "rich and beautiful" girls—and Muff Mobley—left in the meeting room.

Everybody was happy!

Chapter 46

In the Money

After George's country club experience with Sparrow, he decided that no amount of money was worth the humiliation he had suffered. He told Sparrow's daddy, Mr. Grant, that he would not tutor Sparrow any more.

When Hadley found out that George was not tutoring Sparrow any more, he quickly applied for the job and he got it. Hadley didn't even try to tutor Sparrow. He just did all of her work for her.

Hadley told Sparrow to sit behind him in a class they were taking together. When they had a test, he would hold up his paper, and she would copy his answers. This worked perfectly until Sparrow made an "A" on the test.

Hadley got put on probation for assisting Sparrow to cheat, but Sparrow got off scot free.

Brother Wright went to the Dean of Discipline's office and began to rant and rave. He said that his son was a good Christian and that the college was just a den of iniquity.

Brother Wright went into one of his "hellfire and damnation" sermons, and he was so loud that he could be heard on the outside of the building. He was screaming and beating his fist on Dean Sistrunk's desk.

Dean Sistrunk called the campus police. They arrested Brother Wright and charged him with disorderly conduct, and he spent the night in jail. The event was written up in the Nashville paper.

Mary Grace and I thought that Brother Wright got what was coming to him. Christina prayed for him.

Probation was a shock to Hadley. He was accustomed to getting by with whatever he pleased in Pea Ridge.

This is what led to the money making scheme that involved George, Worth, and Hadley.

Unlike George, Hadley worshiped Sparrow, and he would do anything for her. Often, Sparrow would come to Hadley's tutoring session with such a bad hangover that she would lay her head down on the table and go to sleep.

"Hadley, you've got to get me something for this hangover," Sparrow would demand.

Hadley wanted to impress Sparrow so much that he decided to invent a cure for hangovers. He decided that he could do the job much faster if he enlisted the help of George and Worth, who were in the same chemistry class with him.

Hadley didn't want to tell George and Worth exactly why he wanted to invent this hangover cure. He just convinced the other two that when they had the cure, they would all be millionaires before they graduated from college.

All three boys were gifted and talented, and they seemed to succeed in everything they did. They always needed money, and this looked like an easy way to make a lot of money. At any one time, over half of the boys in their dorm were hung over. They put their minds together, and they worked out a formula for a hangover cure.

They started collecting the ingredients they would need: diet pills, No-Doz, and vodka. They bought the diet pills from a plump girl who refused to take the pills. She was happy to get her money back.

Truck drivers always needed to stay awake so they could make as many miles as they could, so the boys went down to Lakeview Truck Stop and bought a lot of No-Doz—more than they could get at a drug store.

Worth stole the vodka from his daddy. He poured half of his daddy's vodka into two fruit jars, and then he filled his daddy's vodka bottles up again with water.

They started selling their concoction to the boys in their dorm. They had a plain formula that they sold for $1.00 a dose, and a deluxe formula that they sold for $1.10 a dose. The deluxe formula was the plain formula, plus three-fourths cup of tomato juice and half a cup of Royal Crown Cola.

The boys were making more money than they ever had made in their lives. The consumers were delighted. They could party all night, take the concoction, and then feel fine the next day.

When they ran out of vodka, Worth went home to steal more from his daddy. When he got home, he found that his daddy had run out of vodka, but he had two jugs of rot-gut moonshine in the pantry.

Worth followed the same procedure. He poured half of each of the gallon jugs into fruit jars, and he filled the moonshine jugs back up with water.

This caused Worth's mama and daddy to get in a big fight. Worth's mama said that Mr. Barfield was drinking too much. Mr. Barfield usually had three shots of booze before bedtime, but lately, he was taking six shots. Mr. Barfield told his wife that it was impossible to get good moonshine any more—you couldn't even get a good buzz by drinking twice the usual amount. It took him a while to figure out that Worth was stealing his booze.

All hell broke loose with the boys when they made their second batch.

Hadley added the correct number of diet pills to the moonshine, but he didn't tell George and Worth what he had done. Worth came along after that, and *he* added the same number of diet pills to the moonshine. Then George, not knowing what the other two had done, came along and added even more diet pills—the number in the formula—to the moonshine.

Now, the concoction was three times as potent, and this resulted in disaster.

The next time Sparrow came to a tutoring session, she was hung over. Hadley gave her some of the hangover cure—from the second batch! Sparrow told Hadley that she had the world's worse hangover, and she needed a double dose. Hadley wanted to please her, so he gave her the double dose.

There was a football game an hour after the tutoring session. Sparrow went over to the stadium to join the cheerleading squad.

By this time, Sparrow had completely lost her mind. She could hardly even walk straight, much less, do her cheers.

By the middle of the second quarter our football team was losing. Sparrow started to throw a fit. "I'm going to have to go out there and help them out," she screamed. And she did.

She ripped off the top of her cheerleader uniform and ran out on the field. She tackled our quarterback, Ruben Stringfellow, who was in the process of passing the football to a wide receiver.

Poor Reuben didn't know what was happening. Here he was, doing what he had always dreamed about—rolling around with a half naked girl. But it was while hundreds of people watched.

The referee stopped the game and started trying to get Sparrow off the field. Mr. Grant ran out on the field to get his "little girl".

If he could have done it, he would have blamed the unfortunate incident on somebody else, but he couldn't. The whole crowd saw what had happened, and it was obvious that nobody had made Sparrow go into a frenzy.

He took Sparrow to the hospital. They put her in a private room, and the doctor on call examined her. He couldn't find anything physically wrong with her, so they put her under observation.

The next morning, after she regained consciousness, the doctor asked her what had happened. Sparrow said that she didn't know, and then she let it slip that she had drunk some of the hangover concoction.

The doctor gave his report to the Dean of Discipline, and Sparrow was expelled from college for one semester. Mr. Grant enrolled her in a Christian college for that semester.

Sparrow returned to our school after being out for that semester, after her daddy wrote a *very* large check to the school's endowment fund.

Chapter 47

The End

Mary Grace, Christina, Alice Ivy, and I all graduated from college and moved to Atlanta. Christina and I got jobs teaching school. Mary Grace and Alice Ivy became airline stewardesses.

George finally figured out that he loved me almost as much as doctoring. Eventually, after he finished medical school, we got married. Then, he went into practice with Dr. Pooten.

Miss Anna finally married Dr. Pooten, but she kept "Green" as her last name.

Miss Lucy hired Hoss as a security guard. He took good care of Miss Lucy and Miss Anna, but now he got paid for it.

Blind Talley kept on panhandling and singing the blues.

Aunt Mazie bought some real flower pots. She also got hot and cold running water, and a television set.

Dusty Silvers married Cherry. Her daddy made him a partner in his business. Then, Dusty ran off with another woman and half of Cherry's money.

Jo Lee married a housing developer. She became an interior decorator and moved back to the south. Jo Lee and I still get together every two or three months for lunch in Nashville.

Little Bitty married Donnie, and they had two beautiful children. She loves being a housewife.

After Lucille married Branton, Sapphire started talking more, and she wasn't so timid. Dr. Pooten and Dr. Green (George) helped her to get fitted for a hearing aid, and this made her personality blossom.

Lee Roy got off scot free because of the circumstances, and he kept on driving those eighteen wheelers.

Worth became a chemist.

Hadley became a science teacher.

Bully took over his daddy's produce business and greatly improved it. He bought his fruits and vegetables from Big 'Un and Big 'Un's brother.

Lou Zena started dating her childhood sweetheart.

Thadamus eventually had to get off of relief. He became a cobbler, and he was very good at it because he loved shoes so much.

Nurse Cleo went to night school and became a real nurse. Her attitude greatly improved.

Coach Posey's wife found out about his affair with Emma Jean Hollowell. Coach's wife divorced him, and that was unheard of in those days.

Trouble discovered that he was good at repairing things. The reform school hired him, and he lived there for years as an employee.

Muff Mobley moved back up north, where she belongs.

Miss Raddle retired. She couldn't function after dealing with the likes of Alice Ivy Green, Sadie Rose Songbird, and Mary Grace Songbird.

Bubba kept on fixing cars.

Esther married Dewey.

Glory moved to Atlanta.

Jackson kept on buying low and selling high, and eventually became a millionaire.

Vernon became an undertaker, like his daddy.

Uncle Alonzo liked the funeral home—he sat with the dead every chance he got. He said that the davenport was comfortable, the food was good, and he enjoyed the company.

Aunt Fern never took drugs again. True to her word, she got Calvin out of the home and put him to work. She changed her will, left all of her money to me, and completely cut Deenie out of the will.

Sparrow married a football player, and Mr. Grant supported his "little girl".

Life goes on pretty much as it always has in Pea Ridge, Tennessee, and every other small town in the American South.

978-0-595-47599-5
0-595-47599-X

Printed in the United States
98001LV00006B/1-48/A